Praise for THE RETRIEVAL ARTIST SERIES

The SF thriller is alive and well, and today's leading practitioner is Kristine Kathryn Rusch.

—Analog

Readers of police procedurals as well as fans of SF should enjoy this mystery series.

—Kliatt

Instant addiction. You hear about it—maybe you even laugh it off—but you never think it could happen to you. Well, you just haven't run into Miles Flint and the other Retrieval Artists looking for The Disappeared. ...I am hopelessly hooked....

—Lisa DuMond
MEviews.com on *The Disappeared*

An inventive plot and complex, conflicted characters increases the appeal of Kristine Kathryn Rusch's *Extremes*. This futuristic tale breaks new ground as a space police procedural and should appeal to science fiction and mystery fans.

—RT Book Reveiws on *Extremes*

Part science fiction, part mystery, and pure enjoyment are the words to describe Kristine Kathryn Rusch's latest Retrieval Artist novel.... This is a strong murder mystery in an outer space storyline.

—The Best Reviews on *Consequences*

An exciting, intricately plotted, fast-paced novel. You'll find it difficult to put down.

—*SFRevu* on *Buried Deep*

A science fiction murder mystery by one of the genre's best…. A book with complex characters, an interesting and unpredictable plot, and timeless and universal things to say about the human condition.

—*The Panama News* on *Paloma*

Rusch continues her provocative interplanetary detective series with healthy doses of planet-hopping intrigue, heady legal dilemmas and well-drawn characters.

—*Publishers Weekly* on *Recovery Man*

…the mystery is unpredictable and absorbing and the characters are interesting and sympathetic.

—*Blastr* on *Duplicate Effort*

Anniversary Day is an edge-of-the-seat thriller that will keep you turning pages late into the night and it's also really good science fiction. What's not to like?

—*Analog* on *Anniversary Day*

Set in the not too distant future, the latest entry in Rusch's popular sf thriller series (*The Disappeared; Duplicate Effort*) combines fast-paced action, beautifully conflicted protagonists, and a distinctly "sf noir" feel to tell a complex and far-reaching mystery. VERDICT Compulsively readable with canny plot twists, this should appeal to series fans as well as action-suspense readers.

—Library Journal on *Anniversary Day*

Rusch offers up a well-told mystery with interesting characters and a complex, riveting storyline that includes a healthy dose of suspense, all building toward an ending that may not be what it appears.

—RT Book Reviews on *Blowback*

We always like our intergalactic politics as truly alien, and Rusch delivers the goods. It's one thing to depict members of a Federation whining about treaties, quite another to depict motivations that are truly, well, alien.

—Astroguyz on *Blowback*

Fans of Rusch's Retrieval Artist universe will enjoy the expansion of the Anniversary Day story, with new characters providing more perspectives on its signature events, while newcomers will get a good introduction to the series.

—Publishers Weekly on *A Murder of Clones*

THE RETRIEVAL ARTIST SERIES:

The Disappeared
Extremes
Consequences
Buried Deep
Paloma
Recovery Man
The Recovery Man's Bargain (Novella)
Duplicate Effort
The Possession of Paavo Deshin (Novella)

The Anniversary Day Saga:

Anniversary Day
Blowback
A Murder of Clones
Search & Recovery
The Peyti Crisis
Vigilantes
Starbase Human
Masterminds

Other Stories:

The Retrieval Artist (Novella)
The Impossibles (A Retrieval Artist Universe Short Story)

SEARCH
&RECOVERY

A RETRIEVAL ARTIST UNIVERSE NOVEL

KRISTINE KATHRYN RUSCH

*wmg*PUBLISHING

Search & Recovery
Book Four of the Anniversary Day Saga

Published 2015 by WMG Publishing
www.wmgpublishing.com
Cover and Layout copyright © 2015 by WMG Publishing
Cover design by Allyson Longueira/WMG Publishing
Cover art copyright © George Tsartsianidis/Dreamstime,
Angela Harburn/Dreamstime
ISBN-13: 978-1-56146-615-3
ISBN-10: 1-56146-615-8

To Colleen Kuehne,
For everything

Acknowledgements

This project is so massive that there is no way I could have done it without the assistance of Annie Reed, Colleen Kuehne, Judy Cashner, and Allyson Longueira.

Special thanks to my husband, Dean, for keeping me sane as the books morphed and changed and grew.

But…I reserve my deepest gratitude for all you readers. Thank you for coming with me on this journey—and for waiting while I completed the books. Your support has sustained me while I wrote. Thank you.

Author's Note

Dear Readers,

This book is the reason that I had to write all of the books in the Anniversary Day Saga before I released any more of them. This book and the next four. Before I explain that cryptic bit of information, let me address all of you in general.

If you are new to the Anniversary Day Saga, back up and start with the book titled Anniversary Day. *If you're new to the Retrieval Artist series, start with any book up to (and including)* Anniversary Day. *The first book in the entire series,* The Disappeared, *is probably best for you to start with, but all of those previous novels stand alone as, I hope, the novels after this saga will as well.*

For those of you who have been with me all along and picked up this book without reading the rest of the saga, here's what's going on: WMG Publishing reissued Anniversary Day *and* Blowback *in the fall of 2014, with new covers and new author's notes inside (no new material, though, so if you've read them, you don't need to scan through the reissues).*

In January of 2015, WMG released A Murder of Clones, *the third book in the saga. This novel,* Search & Recovery, *is the fourth book in the saga, and it appeared in February of 2015. The rest of the books in the saga will be released one per month in 2015 through June, when the last book in the saga will appear. For more information about the saga and the series, go to retrievalartist.com.*

Here's why you're getting six books in six months:

I write stories out of order. I have always done so, for reasons I don't entirely understand. Usually, though, my stories are contained in one novel that wraps up at the end, so before I release the novel into the world, I can put it in order. But when I write an entire saga, the saga is the story, not the novels that create the saga.

And in the past, traditional publishing schedules only allowed for one series book per year, so writing something like the Anniversary Day saga was almost impossible to do well.

When I started Anniversary Day, *I had no idea that it would take so many books to finish the long arc. As I look at the story I was trying to tell, though, it makes sense. You can't—well, I can't—write about a vast epic in one or two novels and feel satisfied. I know some writers can, but honestly, I don't much care for those books.*

So, following the rule that all writers should follow, I'm writing a story I would like to read. It's long, it's involved, but it does follow a plan and an arc. I just had to write around various parts of the puzzle until I figured out exactly what the entire saga needed.

And I'm glad I waited to publish until I finished the rest of the saga. Because this is the book that reminded me why I chose to publish after *I finished.*

Search & Recovery didn't exist until I had nearly finished the book I initially thought of as the third book in the Anniversary Day saga—The Peyti Crisis. The Peyti Crisis (which is the March book) will feature Miles Flint. I thought I had finished The Peyti Crisis in January of 2014, but something bothered me about it, something that I couldn't put my finger on.

Then I started the next book in the saga, Vigilantes, *and characters kept showing up, telling me what they had done on the way to the Moon. I figured I could write really boring "and this happened and this happened" dialogue, or I could write the actual stories.*

Besides, at that moment, all of the villains revealed themselves, with some surprises, and I realized that I needed to understand why they did what they had done. I had a vague idea, but when you're writing a long story arc, a vague idea wouldn't be very satisfying.

I know I write out of order, and I knew the end of this saga was being written out of order. If I were still working in traditional publishing, out of New York, I would have written one or two books a year on this series for the next few years, and felt very frustrated when I realized I had told the middle section wrong.

I would have figured out how to make it work, but it would have felt like walking backwards in a windstorm. WMG Publishing has given me the freedom to write the story arc I want to write (which is essentially one giant book split into novel-sized chunks) and to publish the novels quickly so you folks don't have to remember year to year what's going on. That freedom makes all the difference in the world.

What this publishing schedule does for the saga is keep it unstuck in time, which is how it should be. Flint and his team were surprised by what happened on Anniversary Day. I had to preserve that surprise, while showing how the crisis unfolded and why. That's why A Murder of Clones (January), this book, and the upcoming Starbase Human (May) are set in the saga's recent past.

Search & Recovery is set shortly after Anniversary Day. The next book, The Peyti Crisis, returns to the days just after Blowback, when all the residents of the Moon must deal with the second attack that hit so soon after the first.

I am conscious that each book needs a beginning, middle, and an end. So even though the saga threads remain unresolved in these middle books of the saga, I'm trying to tell smaller stories within the larger one.

This is one of those smaller tales. I hope you enjoy it.

—Kristine Kathryn Rusch
Lincoln City, Oregon
May 31, 2014

SEARCH
&RECOVERY

A RETRIEVAL ARTIST UNIVERSE NOVEL

FOUR YEARS AGO

1

Berhane Magalhães's mother put her arm around Berhane's shoulder, pulled her close, and kissed the top of her head. Berhane flushed, but refrained from looking around the *Armstrong Express* car at the other passengers to see if they noticed her mother's inappropriate display of affection. Berhane used to glance at others guiltily when she was younger, and all it would do was make her mother's trilling laugh echo through whatever compartment they were in.

This compartment was large and wide, with silver built-in seats that accommodated most two-legged species, and some sideways booths for wider aliens. There was even a flat tabletop area for the Disty. A Disty sat cross-legged on it now, its tiny childlike shape belying its ferocity.

Berhane had grown up fearing the Disty. Apparently, her father had lost business associates to them, and he loved to talk about how awful the Disty were and how they murdered indiscriminately. *Earth Alliance law allowed for it*, he would say, and then he would add, *That's such a travesty.*

She tried not to look at the Disty—and found herself looking at a wide variety of humans instead. They were standing, sitting, watching vids on their links, swaying to the train's movement. Scattered among them, a few Peyti—gray aliens so thin that they looked like they would shatter with a tap to their twig-like arms. They wore masks over much of their faces, which she had grown used to in her time at the university.

3

Berhane hadn't had a lot of contact with aliens before she graduated from the Armstrong Wing of the Aristotle Academy two years ago. Now, aliens filled her classes, and the hallway, and the public transportation she took daily to get to Dome University's Armstrong campus.

Apparently, Berhane's mother noted her discomfort with the aliens and pulled Berhane even closer. Berhane didn't move away, although she wanted to. Her mother—and probably most of the humans in the car—would have found the movement rude.

And whatever she thought of her mother, Berhane didn't want to be rude to her. She knew they just misunderstood each other most of the time.

Madeline Magalhães believed in laughter and affection and warmth; for some reason, she had married a man who believed in none of those things, leaving her children confused about the very nature of love and proper behavior.

None more than Berhane, who adored her father. He seemed to approve of her, although he rarely said so. But of all the family members, the only one he talked to about business and the future was Berhane.

Her mother grinned at everyone else in the compartment. Most of them looked away. Her mother rarely rode public transportation, but this morning, she was accommodating Berhane—sort of.

Berhane had mentioned that they'd be taking the five a.m. inner dome train in an effort to dissuade her mother from accompanying her. Predictably, her mother had mentioned bringing their own car, but Berhane had vetoed that.

She hated parking in the university lots. Not only was it difficult to find a space, but she found that having a car—particularly one of the most expensive models on the Moon—made her feel less like a student and more like a wealthy dilettante.

"You really need to listen to me," her mother said softly, after she had kissed Berhane's head.

"I do listen," Berhane said a little too loudly. The big man near her looked over. She glared at him, wondering if his size was a conscious choice. He looked wealthy enough to afford thinness enhancements.

4

"My darling," her mother said, laughter in her voice, "you have never listened to me. But you need to, now."

"Mom," Berhane said. "I have finals this week. I don't have time to think about any big life changes."

Whenever her mother got this tone, she wanted Berhane to do something. Change her major, be nicer to her father, talk to her brother about something he was doing wrong.

Given the timing, her mother probably wanted her to break up with her boyfriend. Her mother had never liked Torkild Zhu, believing him to be a cold-hearted bastard like her father. At least, those were her mother's words.

And maybe her mother was right on some level. Torkild wanted to be a lawyer, not because he cared about people, per se, but because he found the law intellectually challenging—and because he thought being a lawyer would be a great way to make money. Not Bernard Magalhães kind of money (one of the richest men on the Moon money), but out-earning your own parents kind of money.

Torkild had said that if he were a lawyer, he would have to answer to himself, the courts, and no one else.

He seemed to think that a good idea. Berhane had not found a way to argue with him.

And she hadn't felt like it. He had his passions; she wished she had hers. She was still looking for her place in the universe. Right now, she was that Magalhães girl, or Torkild's girlfriend, or a Dome University student.

No one knew who Berhane was because Berhane didn't know who Berhane was either.

Her mother's smile vanished. "You need to make time to talk with me. I don't think this can wait any longer."

Drama. Her mother was all about drama—happy drama, but drama nonetheless.

Her mother must have seen the reluctance on Berhane's face. She patted Berhane on the leg.

"Tell you what," her mother said. "I'll stop at the Shenandoah Café and get that cinnamon coffee you like. I'll bring it to your favorite table in the quad in, what? An hour?"

Berhane resisted the urge to roll her eyes. That was what she got for telling her mother her exam schedule. She could almost hear herself blithely nattering last night:

I'm not worried about the first exam, even if it is at 6:30 in the morning. It's Poetry of the New Worlds, which is going to be an essay exam, graded on creativity, which just means repeating the lectures the professor gave that he obviously thought were brilliant...

"I thought you had a meeting," Berhane said, trying not to sound desperate. She hated heart-to-hearts with her mother. "That was what you told me last night."

Her mother's smile was wide and warm, deepening the creases around her eyes and making her seem even more cheerful than usual.

"I do have a meeting," her mother said. "It's with you."

Berhane felt a surge of irritation. Her mother always manipulated her like that. But before Berhane could say anything, her mother stood. The train was slowing. Her mother headed to the nearest exit, along with two Peyti, three Imme, and a short woman who didn't quite block Berhane's view of her mother's face.

Her mother smiled at Berhane, then waggled her fingers. Berhane gave her a reluctant shake of the head. Her mother knew that Berhane was annoyed at her—and in typical fashion, her mother didn't really care.

The train stopped, the door eased open, and the group of seven from this part of the car stepped onto the outdoor platform—although nowhere in Armstrong's dome was really outside. Outside was the Moon itself, with its own gravity and lack of oxygen. Berhane had gone out there several times in an environmental suit, generally with her father on business, and it had always freaked her out.

The platform glowed golden in light from Dome Dawn. Her mother's hair had reddish highlights from the fake sunlight, and her matching black pantsuit glowed reddish as well. She walked to the side of the platform, heading toward the stairs, as the train eased forward.

Berhane felt a longing for cinnamon coffee. The Shenandoah Café made the best in Armstrong. Her mother definitely knew how to bribe her. And after this stupid final, Berhane would want some kind of refreshment, even if it meant letting her mother harangue her.

The train sped up, heading across the famed University shopping district with its funky stores and fantastic restaurants (including the Shenandoah Café), before it reached the first of five University stops. Berhane didn't settle in. She would get off on the second stop and walk less than a block to get to her exam.

Berhane felt annoyed. Instead of focusing on the exam (which was going to count for 75% of her grade), she was thinking about whatever it was that her mother wanted. And it had to be something important (life-changing, her mother had said) to merit cinnamon coffee and a forced meeting.

The train slid sideways.

Berhane's heart rose and her breath caught.

Trains weren't supposed to slide sideways. They couldn't slide sideways.

Berhane felt a surge of alarm.

Then the train car toppled backwards, and the people near the door flew toward her.

A big man landed on her, knocking the wind from her. Screams echoed around her. Beside her, a Peyti—its face grotesque and strange— gasped. It had no mask. It was on its side, groping for its mask with its twig-like fingers. Somehow Berhane managed to grab the mask and give it to the Peyti, all without dislodging the big man on top of her.

More people had landed on him, and the screaming continued.

Then another *thump* occurred, making the car jolt upward as if nothing held it down, not even the weight of the people inside. The car had gone dark.

She managed to catch a thin breath, although it hurt. Then she realized that the air tasted of chemicals. Burned chemicals. She peered through the window, which was now above her, and saw a blackened dome.

The car hadn't gone dark—or maybe it had—but the dome had gone dark too. Domes didn't go dark. That meant the power was off, the environment was no longer being filtered, and everyone would die.

They would all die.

She gasped for air again, her chest aching. The air burned its way down her throat.

She willed herself to think—not about dying, but about surviving. She needed to survive. She needed to live. If she thought about dying, she would, underneath the big man who smelled of sweat, in a closed car filled with screamers, and near a Peyti clutching its mask to its bony little face. Its eyes met hers, and in their liquid depths, she thought she saw panic.

She wouldn't panic. She couldn't.

The car hadn't shifted any more. Whatever had happened was over—at least for the moment.

She moved her arms under the big man, finding his back or his shoulders or some solid part of him, and she shoved.

"We have to move," she said.

She could barely hear herself in all the screaming. The Peyti was still staring at her.

She shoved again.

"Move!" she shouted at the big man, and he did, somehow, sliding toward the seat behind her.

A tangle of people and a Disty tumbled on top of her and she kept shoving.

"Move!" she yelled again, and this time, her voice cut through the screams. The fact that someone (she) had taken charge seemed to galvanize everyone.

People started picking themselves up, rolling away from each other, asking questions instead of screaming.

"Anything broken?"

"You okay?"

"Can you slide this way?"

Berhane tuned out the words and managed to pull herself upright. She was now standing on the window of the car, her back against the ceiling. The train had derailed, something she hadn't thought possible. Weren't they built so that they couldn't derail? She remembered hearing about that in one of her classes. Something about magnetized couplings and nanobots and—

She wiped a hand over her face, and took another deep breath of the chemical-laden air. She was in shock, or sliding into shock, and she didn't dare, because they were trapped in this car. Judging from the smells around her—those chemicals, the stench of burning—something had gone very wrong somewhere, and she couldn't know if it was the train itself or if it was the dome.

The Peyti grabbed her leg. She looked down at the thin gray fingers wrapped around her pants.

"Please," it said.

She reached down, and helped it up. Its other arm dangled at its side, clearly broken. She'd always thought the twig-like Peyti looked fragile. Now she knew that they were.

"Thank you," it said.

"There's something in the air," she said because she knew the Peyti, with its mask, couldn't smell what had gone wrong. "Something bad."

The Peyti nodded and surveyed the area around them. Other survivors were moving, shuffling toward the side of the car.

The Peyti said something in its native language and looked back at her.

"What?" she asked.

It shook its head, a movement that looked very unnatural. It clearly worked among humans and had learned their movements.

"The dome sectioned," it said.

She frowned. "How do you know that?"

"Do not look north," it said.

She didn't even know where north was. She was completely disoriented.

"Oh, my God." The big guy was standing on the seat back beside her. "We got cut in half."

9

Berhane didn't understand him at first. She was fine. Except for broken bones and bleeding, everyone else seemed fine too. She glanced at the big man, then started to turn toward the direction he was looking in, but the Peyti grabbed her arm.

"Do not look," it said. "The dome bisected the train."

Her breath caught. "It can't do that."

"Not under regular circumstances, no," the Peyti said. "The trains must stop when the dome sections, but clearly this is not a regular circumstance."

The dome only dropped its sections when the mayor ordered the dome to get segmented off. He had done so during the crisis surrounding the Moon marathon. He had sectioned off one part of the dome, so the disease running through the marathon didn't infect the rest of the city.

But that was the only time in her memory that the dome had sectioned.

And that sectioning had been *ordered*. Trains had stopped in time. Cars hadn't been able to get through the area. People had been instructed to move away from the section before it came down.

Not this time.

"What happened?" she whispered.

"Something bad," the Peyti said.

The something bad had happened in the forward compartments.

Then Berhane realized she was turned around. The sectioning had occurred behind her.

Where her mother had been.

"No," Berhane said.

She scrambled past the people still picking themselves up, and climbed toward the door. It was half open, something that shouldn't have happened either, or maybe that was a fail-safe when the train derailed (only it wasn't supposed to derail).

Somehow she pried the doors open and squeezed through.

The air was thick with the smell of burnt rubber and fried circuits. Her eyes watered.

She could see the dome behind her, set against the famed university shopping district, but it looked wrong.

Black. Rubble. Smoke, billowing everywhere. Some of it near the sectioned dome, but most of it behind the protective barrier.

She climbed on top of the car. The train was twisted too. Cut in half. Sort of. Because in the back, past the section, she couldn't see a train at all.

She couldn't see anything she recognized.

"Mother," she whispered. And then she shouted, "Mother!"

Her mother never shouted back.

ANNIVERSARY DAY

2

BERHANE TOSSED HER ENGAGEMENT RING AT TORKILD ZHU'S RETREATING back. The ring missed by a good five meters, and bounced on the blue carpet of Terminal 20's luxury departure lounge.

Three employees of the Port of Armstrong stared at her as if she were the crazy one. A little girl ran toward the ring, glinting on the carpet, and her father caught her arm. A Peyti watched, eyes glittering above its mask.

But Torkild didn't turn around. Of course not, the bastard. He probably didn't even know she had thrown the ring at him.

She wiped the back of her hand over her wet cheeks, then blinked, afraid the tears would start again. She doubled over, her face warm. It felt swollen, and her eyes ached.

Damn him. Damn him all to hell.

It was just like Torkild to pick the departure lounge of Armstrong's port as the site of their break-up. He couldn't have done it in the car when she brought him here, or in her apartment.

Or in bed—

Good God, the bastard had made love to her—*screwed* her—just that morning, even though he had known what he was going to do. But he hadn't told her he loved her. He hadn't said that at all, even though she had pressed herself against him and declared her love for him loudly, so that he couldn't ignore her.

At least, in that moment, he had had the decency to look away.

Bastard. Bastardbastardbastard *bastard.*

Somehow her cheeks were wet again, but she wasn't sure if the tears were anger or frustration or humiliation or actual grief.

No, she knew they weren't actual grief. She'd felt grief before. She knew grief, and it hadn't felt like this.

Someone tugged on her arm.

Berhane looked down. The little girl, advertising-cute with her black pigtails, coffee-dark skin, and button black eyes, held the ring in her thumb and forefinger.

"'Spretty," the little girl said, slurring the words together. "Daddy says 'spensive too. Shouldn't throw it."

Out of the mouths of babes.

The little girl's father was standing just to the side. He gave Berhane an apologetic shrug of his shoulders, as if he couldn't control his daughter.

He probably couldn't.

What father could?

"Thank you." Berhane took the ring gently from the child, biting back all of the nasty words she would have said if Torkild were still standing there.

It's not expensive, she would have said. *It's a cheap ring from a true asshole, and he knew it even when he gave it to me.*

Back then, she hadn't cared. Not even when he apologized as he gave her the ring.

I know you can probably afford to buy a million of these, he had said earnestly, *but this is what I can get us on a student's budget. I hope you don't mind.*

Mind? she had replied like the lovesick suck-up she was. *That makes the ring even more special.*

The little girl hadn't moved. She was still looking at the ring, as if she wanted it for herself.

"You okay?" the little girl asked. She was biting her lower lip, and actually seemed concerned as her gaze met Berhane's.

Berhane wondered what the girl's father would do if Berhane gave the child the ring. Probably make her give it back. That was what Berhane's father would have done. But not for the same reason. He would have done it because it was a cheap ring, not worthy of his daughter.

This man would probably give it back because it was the right thing to do.

Still, Berhane was touched that the child asked about her well-being. Berhane gave the girl a watery smile that felt completely insincere.

"Yes, thank you," Berhane said. "I'm fine."

The little girl looked at the ring. "You gonna put it on?"

"Not now," Berhane said, and closed her hand around it. The sharp metal prongs holding the half-carat ruby-like stone in place bit into her palm.

The little girl's face fell, as if a ring shouldn't be treated like that. She scurried back to her father.

Berhane raised her head, her gaze meeting his. He was about her age, as dark as his daughter. His daughter had his black eyes. He raised his eyebrows at Berhane, as if questioning—what? That she was all right? That she hadn't harmed his daughter?

Berhane sighed, then looked at the door leading out of the Terminal. Damn that Torkild. He had deliberately ended their relationship here, so that he wouldn't have to answer to her.

He was a coward, just like Berhane's father had said he was.

He's not worthy of you, my girl, her father had said more than once, and that comment had always made Berhane feel special and pathetic at the same time.

She had felt special because her father had noticed her, and pathetic because she needed him to notice her. And pathetic too because he had criticized her boyfriend, and in doing so, had criticized her as well.

It irritated her that her father had been right. And her mother had been as well. Neither of them had liked Torkild.

Berhane had always suspected her mother wanted to talk with her about Torkild on the day of the bombing, four years ago now.

Dammit.

The man was no longer looking at her. He had his hand on his daughter's shoulder. What were they doing there? Seeing someone off, as she had been doing? Because it was too late to get onto the shuttle to Athena Base.

Berhane had no idea why she was so interested in them. Maybe because the girl had brought herself to Berhane's attention. Or maybe because Berhane couldn't remember ever standing with her father anywhere, waiting for something, just her and her dad.

Except at her mother's funeral. Then they had stood side-by-side, greeting the guests, because Berhane's brother Bertram had been too broken up to talk to anyone. Bert had acted as if he were the only one harmed by their mother's death, as if he were the only one grieving.

He had barely made it through the funeral before screaming at their father. Somehow, the explosion that had killed her mother, an explosion caused by some terrorists connected with a place that Berhane had never heard of before that awful day, had become their father's fault, at least in Bert's eyes. Berhane had never understood the fight.

Their mother had been in the wrong place at the wrong time, and had died for it.

End of story. Sometimes life was like that, much as Berhane hated it. Much as she grieved over it.

Real grief, not the tears she was shedding for Torkild The Terrible. She wiped at her eyes.

Bert had taken his inheritance from their mother and fled to the Frontier, after their father had made him sign off on any interest he had in the family business from that moment forward. Berhane had thought the requirement harsh, but her father had said that it would protect her inheritance and Torkild, the bastard, had agreed.

Berhane ran a finger beneath her eyelid. She probably should leave. She had made a scene after all. Her mother would have been appalled.

No, that wasn't right: her mother would have laughed. Her mother had been the one who hadn't cared about the opinion of others. Her father cared, mostly because he was afraid that a bad opinion would have a negative effect on business.

Berhane glanced at the door, then looked up at the screen hanging behind one of the sign-in desks. It showed the shuttle to Athena Base waiting for the last of its passengers to get settled.

First class always got to go first, and since Torkild's law firm paid his way onboard, Torkild always traveled in the most expensive way possible.

He's only marrying you for your money, my girl, her father had said.

I'm not fond of him, her mother had said after meeting him. *Berhane, you can do so much better.*

How right her parents were. She could have done a lot better—many times over. She had wasted almost a decade of her life on Torkild, waiting for him, trying to set a date, even volunteering to move to Athena Base so that she could live near his work instead of so very far away.

I need an excuse to come back to my home, Berhane. I will come to see you, Torkild had said after he got hired by Schnable, Shishani, & Salehi, the best defense firm in the human part of the Alliance. The hiring had been—in his words—a dream come true. And he wanted to establish himself there before bringing her to that far region of space.

The idea that she was "an excuse" to come home had bothered her, but she had let it slide. She had known what he meant.

Or she'd thought she had.

He would bring her to Athena Base as soon as he felt secure in the law firm. Only, after he had become a junior partner in the firm, he still had excuses.

He doesn't love you, B, Bert had said on one of their infrequent talks over very distant links. *I have no idea what his game is, but he doesn't love anyone. Not even himself.*

She might have believed that—okay, she had believed that (a little) when she was getting her second doctorate. Torkild needed her father's name and his corporate backing, just as clout, to help him with his job at S3. But after he became a partner? He didn't need her or her clout or her family's name.

Not that the Magalhães name meant much outside of Earth's solar system. She had tried to explain that to Bert too, but he hadn't listened.

Everyone's heard of us, he said bitterly in one of their conversations. *Even way out here, I can't escape Dad's reputation.*

Bert wanted to escape their father. Berhane did not. She even hated leaving Armstrong. She couldn't imagine living off-Moon.

She was still staring at that stupid shuttle. What had she been thinking? She was holding things up as much as Torkild was. She didn't want to leave the Moon, and he didn't have a future here.

Maybe he was just being realistic when he broke up with her.

Or maybe he was just being a bastard.

She almost chucked the damn ring at the door again. It took all of her strength to keep from flinging that flimsy token of an even flimsier love at the stupid blue carpet.

Instead, she looked at the ring in her palm, saw the indentations it made against her skin, then noted that she had similar marks on her left ring finger. It would take a long time before evidence of that stupid ring would wear off.

She balanced the ring on her palm. She had no idea what she would do with that ring. Torkild had been right: she could buy a million of these things with her monthly allowance, not even touching the principal of her inheritance from her mother, not to mention the money she got from her father every month.

The ring was just a symbol of her stupidity.

She closed her fist around it again, then walked over to the man and his daughter. He looked at her in surprise.

The little girl looked at Berhane's hand, as if searching for the ring.

Berhane opened her fist quickly, above the girl's head, and showed the man the ring.

"You saw what happened," she said softly to him. "I don't want this. Someone else is intrigued with it."

And she pointedly looked down at the top of the little girl's head.

"It's too expensive," the man said.

Berhane smiled bitterly. "You don't know who I am, do you?"

He frowned. "Should I?"

"I'm Berhane Magalhães, Bernard Magalhães's daughter. I thought I was marrying for love, not for money, which is why I ended up with this ring." She paused, and the man held up his hand.

"This isn't about me," he said.

"I know," she said. "I'm telling you who I am so that you'll know this ring is—"

To tell him that the ring was cheap in her estimation was elitist, and she only realized it when the sentence was halfway out of her mouth.

"Sorry," she said. "It's just that I'm not going to keep this. I could sell it, but that seems silly. I'd rather give it to someone who'll find it special."

His gaze stayed on hers. Then he let out a small laugh.

"You realize that some psychiatrist would say that, because you couldn't give the ring back to your fiancé, you're looking for a substitute to give the ring to."

She let out a small laugh too. She couldn't help herself.

"That psychiatrist would probably be right," she said, shaking her head at herself. She hadn't even realized it until this nice man pointed out what she was doing.

But she couldn't go back on it now.

And she didn't want to.

"I doubt," she said, "that someone under the age of five qualifies as that substitute."

The man gave her a sideways you're-not-fooling-me glance. His daughter was looking up as if she could see what was on Berhane's palm. At the mention of age, the girl's eyes lit up.

"Now you've done it," the man said lightly.

Berhane nodded. "Not as cagey as I thought, I guess."

The man sighed, and scanned his daughter. She was shifting on her small feet, looking hopeful, glancing between her father and Berhane's outstretched palm.

It was hard to miss how interested she was.

He sighed, then said, "I want to record you offering it to my daughter. Before you do, you have to tell her—and me—that you're doing it because you want to."

Berhane appreciated his caution. The last thing he needed was a jilted fiancée changing her mind about the token of that (horrible) affection. Not to mention deciding that this random man and his daughter, here in the Terminal, could be accused of stealing the ring.

"No problem," Berhane said. "I'm happy to do it. Are you ready to record?"

He blinked, and the pupil of his right eye glowed for a second.

"Yes," he said.

"Okay," Berhane said. "I'm Berhane Magalhães. I am giving this ring of my own free will to….?"

She looked at the man. He said, "Fiona Ó Brádaigh."

"To Fiona Ó Brádaigh," Berhane said, then she crouched. The little girl—Fiona—was bouncing on her toes with excitement. "And I hope you'll love and enjoy it for the rest of your very long life."

The little girl took the ring as if it were the most precious thing she'd ever seen. She tried to slip it on her finger, but it was several sizes too big. She could fit two of her fingers into the ring.

Berhane reached around her neck and removed her necklace. It was just a chain with a charm at the bottom of it, something whimsical she had bought a few weeks ago on break from one of her classes.

She pulled the charm off, pocketed it, and then extended her hand.

"Let me," she said to the little girl.

The girl clutched the ring.

"She's trying to help, Fee," the girl's father said. "Let her put it on the chain."

The little girl gave the ring back, lips thin, as if she expected Berhane to keep the ring again. Instead, Berhane slipped the ring through the chain, then hung it around the little girl's neck.

The chain was still too big. It extended to the bottom of the little girl's rib cage. The girl clutched the ring as if she would never let it go.

"What do you say, Fee?" the man asked.

The little girl looked at Berhane, whose cheeks were flushing again.

The child didn't trust her. Of course not. Her relationships—

Then the girl launched into her arms, hugging her tightly. "Thank you, thank you, thank you," she whispered in Berhane's ear, then pulled away so fast that Berhane felt breathless.

The girl clung to her father's leg.

Berhane stood.

"That was a kindness," he said. "You didn't have to do that."

"I know," Berhane said. "But I've learned—well, it doesn't matter. I should be thanking you both for making this morning a little easier."

The girl looked at her, hand still clutching the ring.

The man smiled at her—a real smile for the first time.

"I hope the universe is nicer to you after today," he said.

"Thank you," she said. "I'll be all right. I think it'll end up being a kindness for both of us."

"Wish I could have your optimism about things," the man said. "It's a gift."

"No," she said. "It's hard earned."

And then she walked away. Somehow she'd figure out how to put Torkild behind her.

She needed to.

3

Luc Deshin sat cross-legged on the hand-woven rug, shoes off, palms resting against the soft wool. The rug was worth more than his house—each of the rugs in this large room was worth more than his house. In fact, everything in here was so expensive that he was afraid to sneeze.

He was sitting with nearly one hundred of the most important business leaders on the Moon. Some (all) were considered shady, and a good ten percent (like himself) were considered more crime lord than legitimate businessman.

Yet no authority had ever been able to pin anything on any of them, no matter how hard someone tried.

In fact, most city governments left them alone, particularly here in Yutu City. Yutu City welcomed them like no other city government on the Moon had in the past.

This facility was testament to it. A series of meeting rooms, all hidden under arches and minarets, served as Yutu City's main conference center, even though the facility belonged to a private company run by Ghodrat Kerman.

This year, Kerman was running the entire meeting, and he was making certain no one would forget it. He also made sure everyone here knew how important he was, and to Kerman, important meant wealthy.

Deshin didn't like ostentatious displays of wealth.

And he considered everything in this large room, with its individual rugs for all of the participants, ostentatious. And they hadn't even gotten to the food service yet. Kerman had promised the best meal this group had ever eaten.

Deshin doubted anyone could live up to that claim: he'd eaten spectacular food all over the known universe. But he knew that the Gathering, which had no official name attached to it, had a competitive streak when it came to meals. Each participant wanted to prove to the others that he was wealthier than all of them and had better taste.

Fortunately, Deshin had organized the Gathering a decade ago and hadn't hosted it since its early years, before every aspect of it became so competitive.

He would stop coming if he didn't get so much business done right here, every single quarter.

He wasn't sure he liked this conference center, though. It was made of compacted Moon clay, which was covered with dyed Moon sand tiles made in the Bay of Rainbows. Yutu City had many ties to the Bay of Rainbows, even though they were not officially sister cities.

Yutu City was on the southeastern side of the Mare Imbrium, about as far as it could get from the Bay of Rainbows and still be part of the Mare Imbrium section of the Moon.

Deshin preferred the Bay of Rainbows. It was a lovely city that took its fanciful name seriously. Yutu City had simply built up from an ancient colony and, like Armstrong, had lovely sections and sections so dilapidated that he felt dirty just walking into them.

This section was neither, although it contained some of the most arresting architecture in Yutu city. The neighborhood had covenants that required only Moon-based materials be used in the buildings. That led to a lot of compacted clay and Moon brick structures, except in this block, where the Moon sand tiles had become part of the design.

Many who lived in Yutu City thought this area a disaster waiting to happen, because some of the building codes were lax to accommodate the covenants. Most people thought the Moon-based materials were weak, especially when it came to beams and struts.

But Deshin had legally invested in many of the building companies that focused on Moon-only products, and he believed in them so strongly that he had built his own home in Armstrong from the materials.

Still, the conference room's small dome arching above him, its supports hidden in the gold and green design, made him uncomfortable. He felt like he was sitting in the middle of some kind of target—both outside and in.

Normally, he didn't think about dome structure—he lived and traveled inside domes all the time—but he was aware that the huge domes protecting the Moon's cities had an intricate structure—and parts that sectioned (and supported) each dome whenever there was a problem.

He doubted there were any sectioning parts in this conference center's small dome. It was a marvel of engineering, but not one he was comfortable sitting under.

He was careful not to look up. He was trying to pay attention to Kerman's welcoming speech, but Deshin's fascination with the dome clearly showed him how hard paying attention was.

It didn't help that Kerman had gone on for fifteen minutes now. Generally, the welcoming speeches at the Gatherings weren't speeches at all. They were simple greetings, followed by all of the instructions that the participants needed to make it through the three-day conference.

Deshin's back ached. He wasn't used to sitting like this, and he had to figure out how to get off the floor without looking like a weak old man. He wasn't weak in any way; he was in the prime of his life. But he wasn't limber anymore, particularly when sitting cross-legged.

He looked around the room. His security team ringed him. For every single person in this room, there were five members of their personal security, not to mention the crowd outside. It looked like some army had bivouacked here.

Back in the days when he had organized the Gathering, he had wanted the participants to leave their security at the hotels, but no one had.

He hadn't either. You didn't invite criminals and shady business people to meetings and expect them to behave well.

Now, as he looked past his team, he saw dozens of people he recognized. While Kerman droned on, Deshin made a list of the appointments he already had scheduled, the short contacts he would try to make, and the handful of rivals he needed to warn off.

He would have a busy conference—and he had no idea what the others who were here would ask of him. He expected to have very little free time after this opening session ended.

He picked his hands off the carpet and rested his wrists on his knees. Sometimes—like this morning—the Gathering felt like a waste of his time, and sometimes it was the most valuable thing he did.

He had started it for everyone he knew whose businesses had both legal and illegal components. If the police ever asked what the group was doing here, they would say they were networking, and they wouldn't be lying. They *were* networking. In the early days, everyone had been trying to figure out how to make illegal businesses look like legal ones.

Now, everyone was trying to figure out how to marginalize the profitable illegal businesses so that they didn't threaten the profitable legal ones.

He almost smiled. He loved the problems that came from success.

Kerman said something about lunch and Deshin looked up, finally focusing on the man who had organized this quarter's meeting.

Kerman stood in the middle of the group. His turban seemed unusually elaborate, and it matched his gold trousers. In fact, everything had gold trim, including the edges of Kerman's kaftan. He wore rings on each finger, and they caught the light as he gestured.

He was barefoot and he even had rings on his toes, which made Deshin look away again. He could barely sit cross-legged. He couldn't imagine walking barefoot, his toes separated by bits of metal.

Then he smiled inwardly. He wasn't squeamish about most things, but he was squeamish about wearing rings on his toes. His wife, Gerda, would make fun of him if she knew about this. His son Paavo would be surprised to learn that his father had a weakness, even such a small one.

Deshin exhaled at the thought of his son. One day, his brilliant boy would realize that his father wasn't half as smart as he was, that Deshin was just pretending to be smarter than Paavo was.

That wasn't entirely true: Deshin was smart about the street, about people, and about business. But when it came to engineering and learning and books, Deshin wasn't smart at all. He admired Paavo and his ability to absorb any fact, all bits of knowledge, without using AutoLearn or his links.

He—

Mr. Deshin?

Luc?

Mr. Deshin?

Sir?

Mr. Deshin?

—an image flashed across his vision: Arek Soseki, the Mayor of Armstrong, sprawled in front of O'Malley's Diner in Armstrong, face gray, clearly dead. The image multiplied into a dozen images and scrolled along the bottom of his vision.

His emergency links had activated. His brain was finally able to separate out the voices from the visual contacts. He blinked, organized them by priority, then looked over the scroll at the room.

Some people were standing. Others had their hands to their ears. Kerman was threading his way between the rugs, heading to the tapestries on the wall, tapestries that Deshin suspected hid doors that Kerman generally didn't want the conference goers to know about.

Normally, Deshin would have stood at the moment his emergency links got activated. He would have left the building to find a quiet place to handle his business.

But everyone here was disrupted, involved in their own personal crisis.

Deshin took a moment to catch his breath, and let the information sink in. He had a lot of projects—both legitimate and illegitimate—with the Mayor of Armstrong. He'd spent a lot of money cultivating their relationship.

He hadn't liked Soseki, but he had found him useful.

And now, Soseki was dead.

He looked at his colleagues. They all would have a different reaction to Soseki's death. The Mayor of Armstrong wielded a lot of power on the Moon, and now he was no more.

Some in here would be trying to manipulate the next election, even though no one knew when that would be held. Others would be trying to make some instant money off the death.

Then Deshin remembered: It was Anniversary Day, the anniversary of the bombing in Armstrong four years ago. He had no idea if that was a coincidence or not.

He doubted it, and that made his stomach clench.

Deshin had family in Armstrong. He needed to know what was happening—not just for his business, but also for the people he loved.

He hunched forward and answered the only voice that mattered to him: his wife Gerda's.

Where are you? he sent. *Are you all right?*

I'm at home, she sent back. *But they're saying the Mayor was assassinated. Paavo's at school…*

The Armstrong Wing of the Aristotle Academy, the most prestigious school on the Moon. Also the most expensive. The place where children of the rich, famous, and powerful went to school.

If someone were targeting important people, then they might go after Aristotle Academy.

And he was hours away, unless he got some kind of emergency shuttle to land here. Dammit, he had taken the bullet train.

He stood and started threading his way through the tangled legs and hunched bodies of his colleagues. A few of them looked at him as he passed, their faces slack with shock.

A death like Soseki's—an assassination, on the Moon, in the middle of Anniversary Day commemorations—would have terrible ripple effects even if no one else was targeted.

I'll order a security team to the school, he sent, and shuddered. His five best security operatives were here, protecting him.

In fact, he corrected, *I'll send as much security as I can. That school needs protecting.*

His team was following him, all dealing with the unfolding crisis on their links. Keith Jakande, the best security operative Deshin had ever had, grabbed him by the elbow and hustled him toward the door.

Deshin turned to him, snapped, "Push much harder and I'm going to fall."

"We have to go, sir," Jakande said. "There's a crisis—"

"I know," Deshin said, but he let Jakande pull him through the growing crowd to a side door Deshin hadn't even known existed. The three men on this security team were all large, "grown on Earth," his wife liked to say, because they had a solidness that was common on Earth and harder to find in anyone who had traveled or grown up in space.

They made Deshin feel small.

The smaller members of the team, both female, were covering his back. Usually the smaller members of his security team disappeared into crowds, but right now, all five were protecting him.

It took Deshin a moment to remember that he was considered someone important in Armstrong as well. If they—the mysterious "they"— were targeting the power structure in Armstrong, of course they would come after him.

And his family.

His heart was pounding, his mouth dry.

He wasn't afraid—he rarely felt fear—but he was getting angry.

He sent for the teams to go to Aristotle Academy through his links, then told Jakande through their private links to make sure the best people were heading there.

"I sent the best team to your home," Jakande said, sounding worried.

The choice: Gerda or Paavo. Deshin's heart constricted.

"It's all right," he said. "Just send a lot of people to that school."

He had a hunch other important parents would be sending their security teams to the academy as well.

He hoped. Because he couldn't get home fast enough to protect any-one. They were on their own, and he had to trust his staff to protect the people he valued the most.

4

BERHANE WAS NEARLY TO THE EXIT OF THE LUXURY DEPARTURE LOUNGE when a red warning label crossed her links. Voices echoed in her head at the same time, and images appeared on all the screens.

Until further notice, The Port of Armstrong has been locked down by order of the Armstrong Police Department.

She stopped walking, just like everyone around her did. She looked toward the nearest screen while sending a request for clarification through her links.

Screens appeared on all the walls, including some screens that had been hidden. The images on the screens alternated. One screen carried information about the closure notification, while the screen next to it showed the exterior of O'Malley's Diner near the port. The exterior views came from overhead. A few tried to show the ground, but hands blocked the cameras, and then those cameras winked out.

"What the—?" asked a woman next to her.

Berhane shook her head. She had no idea. She'd been to O'Malley's a million times, usually with her father at some fundraiser. In fact, she normally would have been with her father right now at some other location, at a speech the governor-general was giving for the Anniversary Day commemorations.

Berhane hated Anniversary Day. She would rather ignore the fact that on this day, her mother had been blown to bits by Etaen terrorists—or someone associated with them. The bomber had never been caught.

The bomb had blown a hole in the dome, and if the sections hadn't come down, everyone would have died.

Berhane still had nightmares about that train, about the blood she'd seen, the bisected car—and the rubble where her mother had been. The smell of burnt electronics still gave her the shudders.

"Do you know what's happening?" a man asked her.

She turned. It was the man she had spoken to a few minutes before. He had his daughter, little Fiona, in his arms. His right hand held her head in place. He clearly didn't want her to see this.

"I'm not getting anything on my links," Berhane said.

"The mayor's been murdered," someone said across the terminal.

Reaction rumbled through the crowd, everyone talking at once. Berhane's stomach clenched.

Of course. O'Malley's. Another Anniversary Day commemoration. Mayor Arek Soseki lived for that stuff. He loved glad-handing people. He never seemed to think about the lives lost—not anymore.

Then she caught herself.

She *knew* Arek. He was dead?

"That can't be true," she said. "I would know."

But how would she know? She was her father's daughter, not her father.

An employee with the port stood on one of the departure desks. He was a slender man in a Space Traffic Control uniform.

"Listen," he said. "I've got confirmation. The mayor was murdered this morning, and they're searching for his killer. The port's in lockdown until further notice. I'm sure it won't take long. They just need to make certain that whoever attacked him didn't board any of the outgoing ships…"

"Dammit," the man beside Berhane said softly. "I don't want Fee in the middle of this. Is there a lounge around here or someplace that'll be quiet?"

"There's a children's area on the second floor of this departure lounge." She knew because she'd come here so many times with her family, especially when she was younger. "Come on. I'll show you."

She pushed her way through the crowd, all of whom were staring at the screens or listening to the Space Traffic employee.

"…like this before. It usually takes an extra hour. We're sorry for the inconvenience…"

She led the man up a flight of stairs. He kept pace with her. No one else was going up. A lot of people and a few aliens were on the other stairway, coming down.

She reached the top of the stairs. Screens danced in front of her, some interacting with her links, all of them showing the exterior of O'Malley's.

Shut off all but emergency links, she sent to her system, just for the moment. She wasn't able to process what was going on—not yet, anyway.

To her left, screens continued. More people, and several different groups of aliens, watched. To her left, the screens vanished. An opaque group of walls protected the children from all the turbulence outside of the children's area.

"It's for babies, mostly, and children who still need daily naps," Berhane said to the man. "But I think they'll let you two inside for a while."

The man was holding little Fiona sideways so that she couldn't see the screens.

"'Swrong?" she asked Berhane.

"I don't know yet, sweetie," Berhane said. "I don't think anyone does. But nothing's wrong with us."

"Nu-uh," Fiona said. "You were crying before."

Of course, she had seen that. Her little hand was still clenched around the ring.

The man's gaze met Berhane's. He was about to say something, but she needed to speak first.

"That man who was talking to me before I met you," Berhane said, "he was mean to me, and made me cry. But you made me smile."

Fiona frowned, as if she didn't understand why. "Me?"

"Yes," Berhane said. "You were nice to me."

Fiona grunted, as if she didn't quite understand that, but she wasn't going to argue with it.

Her father kissed the top of her head.

"You've been kind to us," he said. "I don't know why—"

Berhane waved him silent. She didn't want to talk about it. She wanted to find out what was going on.

"If you ever need anything, not that I can probably help you with anything, considering," he said, "but if you do, I'm Donal Ó Brádaigh. I was just here to say good-bye to someone. I live in Armstrong."

He probably knew that she lived in Armstrong as well.

"Thank you," she said. "I'll remember that."

She hoped she didn't sound too dismissive. She wasn't going to ask him for anything, ever. She didn't do things like that.

She nodded toward the children's area. Another parent, two toddlers in tow, hurried inside.

"I suspect you won't have to wait long," she said.

"Thank you," he said again. "Wave good-bye, Fee."

Fiona didn't let go of the ring. But she whispered, "Bye."

Then the man—Donal—took Fiona into the children's area without looking back.

Berhane watched them for a moment. While waiting for that bastard Torkild, she had waited to have children too. Although that probably wasn't entirely fair. She had told Torkild she wasn't sure she ever wanted children.

She hadn't been ready to think about them.

And she certainly wasn't ready now.

She sighed, then turned around. The image on the screens was all the same now. A close-up of Arek's face. He didn't look like himself. He almost looked like a stone visage of the mayor, toppled over and somewhat off.

Her breath caught in her throat. She'd liked Arek, even if she had thought him a bit of a media whore. He had helped her with some charity work, even when her father had opposed wasting the time.

Her father's favorite criticism: wasting time.

Which she was doing, looking at Arek now. Dead. On Anniversary Day.

She wiped her hand over her face, surprised that the tears had stopped. Her skin was sticky, though. She needed to find a bathroom and splash some water on her cheeks.

There was probably a bathroom on this floor, but she didn't want to thread her way through the crowd. Instead, she went back to the stairs.

As she did, she realized that her father might not have heard what was going on. He hated to be interrupted when he was at an event, and unless the governor-general had made an announcement, no one at the speech had probably heard.

Berhane reinstated all of her links. Aside from the messages from the port assuring her that things would be settled soon, she had received nothing.

Dad? She sent along her links.

She took the stairs down.

She got nothing in response, which was odd. She boosted the audio and established a written link as well, just in case she couldn't hear. The conversation in the luxury terminal was louder than she had ever heard before.

Dad, it's important.

She still got no response. Not an image, not some kind of *Bernard Magalhães has no link access. Your message will remain in the queue until access is restored*—none of the usual brush-off messages.

Nothing.

Her heart started to pound. She couldn't remember where the governor-general was giving her speech. It was in Armstrong, right? Not Littrow, which was where the newly formed United Domes of the Moon had established itself.

Daddy, Berhane sent, this time through the family's emergency links. *Contact me now. I don't know if you got the news about Arek, but I'm worried. It's Anniversary Day…*

And all of this was echoing for her. How many messages had she sent to her mother that long, long morning exactly four years ago?

She couldn't lose both parents on the same day, four years apart, could she?

And had Torkild actually thought it through, breaking up with her on *this* day? The bastard.

She let out a breath. Anger. Good. It was better than panic and fear.

She stopped halfway down the stairs and scanned the lower part of the luxury terminal, although she wasn't sure what she was looking for.

There was nowhere to pace now. All of the aisles were filled with people and aliens, standing, staring at the imagery coming on the floating screens. Other passengers remained in their comfortable chairs, hands pressed against their ears the way that humans did when they were trying to focus on information inside their links. A few Peyti lingered near the doorways, heads tilted as they got information, their masks elongating their faces, their sticklike hands at their sides.

There weren't a lot of non-humans in the lounge, which was probably a good thing. The xenophobia in Armstrong had grown ever since the bombings, and the crazies often came out on Anniversary Day.

Obviously.

She had stopped in front of five screens. She couldn't avoid the images—the mayor, sprawled; the police, talking, moving, unable to figure anything out. No visuals from wherever the governor-general was giving her speech, not yet.

People passed her, hurrying down the stairs as if there was actually somewhere to go. She leaned against the railing, trying to catch her breath.

She needed to think.

Her father was probably fine. He was either listening to a speech he didn't want to hear or he was securing his business interests in the wake of another attack in the city.

Her gaze went to Arek's face again, only visible on one screen now. Two other screens showed the police, conferring, and yet another showed imagery from the speech Arek had given not an hour ago.

She ran a hand over her face.

This concerned her only as a citizen of Armstrong. A survivor of Anniversary Day. A casual friend of Arek.

Nothing more.

Sad as it all was.

She took another deep breath and forced herself to feel calm. Just because everyone else was panicking didn't mean she had to.

She stood up and was about to continue down the stairs when the doors to Terminal 20 opened.

Travelers flooded in, looking angry, harried, sad, confused. It looked like a large ship had arrived, but one hadn't. There'd already been an announcement that nothing would land, or at least let the passengers disembark, until this crisis was over.

So everyone who came in was from the ships that had been about to leave.

She couldn't help herself; she looked for Torkild.

And hated herself for doing so.

5

THE TEAM PUSHED LUC DESHIN OUT OF THE BUILDING. HE WAS STUMBLING beside others from the Gathering, all looking inward, communicating on links.

His stomach was in knots. He wanted to contact Paavo, but knew he would just upset the boy. The school would handle things well; they always did.

And his people would be there soon. Once they arrived—once they contacted him—he would let Gerda know.

She had to be worried too.

The light from Yutu City's dome was amber. They didn't try to mimic Earth days here, but invented their own weird coffee- and tea-like colors that seemed to rotate randomly.

He hated it. It felt alien, and he didn't like anything that felt alien. He liked to be in control of his environment. He didn't like having it control him.

The air outside smelled worse than it had inside the building. Sweat and some kind of exhaust from equipment that would have been illegal in Armstrong. Not to mention the dome environmental filters, salted with something scented—some kind of incense, maybe, or a faint perfume. Scenting the air was also illegal in Armstrong.

It made him lightheaded—all of this was making him lightheaded.

He wanted to go home more than he ever had in his entire life.

"We need some kind of transport," he said to Jakande.

"The good ones have already been hired, sir," Jakande said.

"Then buy us one, for God's sake," Deshin snapped.

Jakande didn't respond. He didn't have to. Deshin knew the man was working his links, even as he moved Deshin forward.

Deshin didn't ask where they were going. They were moving in a group of people who had emerged from the Gathering, all with personal agendas, all focused now on Soseki's assassination and its aftermath, not on any business that would have happened here.

I need a report from my teams, he sent back to his office in Armstrong. *I need to know that my son is all right.*

Team on the ground at the academy, sir, sent the acting head of security. *Your son and his classmates are protected. The school is protected.*

"How's that transport coming?" Deshin asked Jakande.

"Private transports aren't fast enough," he said. "At least, not the ones left. We're taking one of the trains. Yutu City has just added three bullet trains to the schedule, figuring that people will want to return to Armstrong quickly."

They were right about that. He liked it when a government actually did some thinking.

He let his team pull him forward—the train station wasn't that far from here, and it looked easier to run/walk the distance than try to negotiate the roads and skyways.

It seemed like every vehicle in Yutu City was clogging the skyways and the streets. The buildings were too close together for Deshin anyway, but when he looked up and saw dozens of vehicles directly above him, he felt claustrophobic.

That and the amber light and the unfamiliar streets made him feel even more uneasy. Or maybe it was Soseki's death.

Deshin had come to some agreements with Soseki—things Soseki's regular constituents probably wouldn't want to know about, but agreements that would benefit Armstrong in the end.

Now, Deshin had no idea what would happen. Soseki had promised to make those agreements happen. There had been nothing recorded, because both men had felt recording their alliance would be risky.

Deshin hadn't expected a vibrant man with a good staff, a man ten years younger, to die so suddenly.

That kind of thing happened on Earth in the bad old days or out on the Frontier or at the edges of the known universe. It happened in alien cultures or corporations with bad owners. It didn't happen on settled places, established places, like the Moon—

Sir?

Mr. Deshin?

Sir?

His emergency links were chattering again. He hadn't revived his regular links, except for Gerda's, and she was being respectful. Silent.

He wasn't sure he liked silent.

More images on the bottom of his vision made him stumble. Jakande held him up.

The images…he had to pull up sound, because the images were just of buildings and hospitals and something (someone) too small for him to see being placed inside some kind of vehicle.

"…Celia Alfreda…"

"…Moon's governor-general…"

"…not sure if she'll survive…"

"What the hell?" he asked, looking around.

"Keep moving, sir," Jakande said tightly.

They weren't far from the station. He could see it from here.

Everything was falling apart in Armstrong. He fully expected to hear that other important figures were dying as well.

Something was very wrong, and he had no idea how to stop it.

6

BERHANE DIDN'T SEE TORKILD IN THE MASS OF BODIES STREAMING INTO the already full lounge. She kept her position near the railing, gripping it as if it were a lifeline.

Then she forced herself to walk down the remaining stairs, slowly.

She wasn't going to look for Torkild any longer. She needed to locate her father, let him know that something awful had happened, and then she had to figure out what she would do next.

The port had released the passengers back into the terminal, which meant that nothing would leave for several hours. Longer than the authorities had said on the links and in their official communications.

She had a hunch something else had gone wrong.

She reached ground level. A Disty bumped her leg, nearly knocking her over. She hadn't seen Disty in here earlier. Clearly, more than one ship had disembarked.

It wouldn't do her any good to remain in the lounge. She needed to leave, maybe go to one of the upscale restaurants nearby, the ones the "peasants," as her father would say, couldn't afford. The fewer people who could afford the place, the greater the privacy she would have.

Then she could try to reach her father again.

She might not be able to leave the port, but she could at least get a meal, locate her father through her links, and figure out what she would do next.

Because going back to school wasn't an option today.

She had had a hunch she wouldn't make it to class anyway. She had thought she'd be drowning her sorrows after seeing her fiancé off for the first time this year. And if things had gone according to Torkild's plan (the bastard), she would be drinking her sorrows away at some bar, trying not to cry because he had dumped her.

For a moment, she regretted giving away the ring. She wanted to fling it another time.

Then she made herself focus on little Fiona's expression when she had received the ring. That had been worthwhile.

Fiona, who was upstairs with her father, hiding out from the news.

It was probably a good thing that they had gone, because this lounge had gotten very crowded. The disembarked passengers were stopping, clogging up the aisles as they stared at the imagery. Others were grabbing their ears, looking shocked. Still others kept moving, acting like they didn't care at all.

They were moving swiftly, some of them trying to leave the lounge. Which they could do. Everyone could do it.

But they wouldn't be able to leave the port until some authority told them it was all right.

Berhane squared her shoulders, trying to stay away from the panicked arrivals.

"Berhane?"

She started. The voice, so close to her, was Torkild's. For half a second, she thought she had her links on audio, and then she realized he was standing right beside her. She could smell his cedar-scented cologne, faint but familiar. He hadn't changed it in more than a decade.

She turned.

He looked a little rumpled and a lot older than he had not an hour before. His coffee-colored skin was lined, and his dark eyes, with their small fold in the corner, were red-rimmed.

He hadn't been crying, had he? He couldn't have been devastated by their break-up. After all, he had wanted it. He had said, *Surely you should have seen this coming, Berhane.*

"If you don't want to talk to me, I understand," he said, and his voice now was mixing with the memory of his voice from earlier in her head. She had to blink to focus. "But I'm hearing something about a murder…?"

He was offering her *sympathy*? What kind of idiot was he?

"Torkild," she said, her tone icy. "It's Anniversary Day. Had you thought that through?"

"They mentioned it as they told us to disembark," he said, and he was clearly oblivious, the idiot. "They're thinking that maybe something bigger—"

"My mother died in the bombing that they're commemorating, had you thought of that?" she snapped.

Torkild caught his breath, looked around at the people streaming around them.

"Here, Berhane?" he asked in a tone that implied *Really? You're doing this now?*

"Yes, here," she said. "You chose this very spot to end our relationship."

"But Berhane, right now—?"

"Yes, right now," she said. "You're the one who started this."

"Berhane, they've evacuated the ships. Something is really wrong here." Suddenly, he was the concerned Torkild, the man she had fallen in love with, not the bastard Torkild, the man the rest of her family thought he was.

But he wasn't concerned for her. He was concerned for himself.

"Yes, something is wrong," she said. "Arek is dead."

She inclined her head toward the screen.

"Arek—?" Torkild didn't know who that was. "Oh, you mean, Soseki. The mayor. You knew him?"

Of course she knew him. She knew everyone who was anyone on the Moon. Wasn't that why Torkild had hooked up with her in the first place?

"Look," she said. "Arek is dead, and I can't reach my father, and you're being an absolute ass. We have to—"

"You can't reach your father?" Torkild frowned. He seemed competent suddenly. Why would he revert to the Torkild she had loved right now? That wasn't fair.

"No, I can't," she said. "I'm hoping it's a problem with the links—"

"Berhane, it's crowded here. Let's go somewhere else."

"There is nowhere else, haven't you figured that out?" she asked. "We can't leave the port."

"I mean inside the port."

Like she had been thinking. Somewhere else inside the port.

"We need to figure this out," he said.

She wasn't sure what *this* was. She wasn't even sure she wanted to figure anything out.

He took her elbow and she shook him off.

"We'll lose each other in the crowd," he said, and grabbed her elbow again. This time she let him hold on, thinking, *Bastard. Bastardbastard-bastardbastard*, just so that she could keep focused on what she hated about him rather than what she liked about him.

He pulled her forward, and she let him.

She let him.

Trailing along behind him just like a dutiful fiancée—

Which she used to be.

7

THE YUTU CITY TRAIN STATION WAS LONG AND BEAUTIFULLY DESIGNED, with minarets whose tips attached to the newest section of the city's dome. Deshin had heard about the conflicts over the tips touching the dome, how much Kerman and his people had spent to be able to break the regulations so that the station's beauty could impress visitors the moment they arrived.

Deshin felt calmer as he got closer to the station. He activated his link with Gerda.

Paavo's safe, he sent.

I know—

He stumbled, fell, the breath knocked out of him. Around him, people were screaming. Buildings were crumbling and the air had turned a dusty gray.

The link to Gerda had broken.

Jakande was on top of him, holding him down. Deshin's ears ached.

"What the—?" he asked aloud, then stopped. He couldn't hear himself, which meant that Jakande couldn't hear him either.

Deshin looked up, saw that the dome had sectioned. The section was a muddy brown and looked like it hadn't been cleaned off since it was built.

He could see people on the other side, also down—the impact of the section colliding with the ground had been worse than the sectioning in

Armstrong four years ago after the bombing there—and it took him a moment to realize that two of his team members were on the other side, one of the men and one of the women.

Do you know what's going on? he sent to Jakande.

Jakande rolled off him but kept a hand on his back, holding him in place. *No, sir.*

Deshin shook him off. *We need to get to that train, right now. They're going to shut down transportation, if they haven't already.*

The other two members of his team could make their own way back. It was one of the risks of working security, that things didn't always go as expected.

They knew it. He knew it.

They had instructions. They would be all right.

He got to his knees and then a *whomp!* knocked him back down. He felt the *whomp!* rather than heard it. A vibration so strong that he wondered if he would ever stand again.

The screaming grew louder, and Deshin was about to grab Jakande, force him toward the station, when he turned.

The area beyond the section was alive with light and fire and smoke. Orange and black and gold, buildings gone, the section streaked with blood and debris.

He let out a small breath or maybe it was a large breath, he had no idea. Just that the area beyond the section was different, that two of his people were in there.

Deshin had no idea how to get them out. They would only have seconds, if that.

Jakande had somehow found his feet and had hurried to the section. Deshin followed. They were almost touching it when yet another *whomp!* knocked them back.

Above them gunshots or something that sounded like them. Deshin looked up, expecting more building to collapse around him.

Instead, he saw chunks of gray brick pelting the dome. It took him maybe five seconds—which felt like five days—to figure out that was bits of building landing on the *exterior* of the dome. The *outside*. Where no bits of the dome should be. No bits of building.

And nothing should fall from above. That was not how the Moon worked.

Then red matter and some liquid spattered on the top of the dome, and Deshin made himself look at the section instead of what was above him.

It took a second for his brain to assemble the pieces into something that made sense.

The dome had exploded.

Or rather, the part of the dome where his people had been. The fires—the red and orange lights—they were gone, and what remained was like a gray dust, a haze he couldn't see through.

Jakande had both fists against the section. He was yelling, but Deshin couldn't hear his individual voice above all the other voices, screaming and screaming and screaming.

Deshin took Jakande's arm and pulled him back. The rest of his team—the remainder of his team—was yelling too.

His best people, forgetting their primary mission. Not because they were bad at what they did, but because this was unthinkable, so they weren't prepared for it, none of them had prepared for it, and only one of them knew how to keep a cool head with the universe burning around them.

Him.

His team was good, but they were *trained*. They hadn't lived through disasters like he had.

We're going to the train, he sent. *And we're going to get that fucker out of this city, even if we have to crash through a section. You got that?*

He pulled Jakande away from the section. Deshin repeated the directive and then took off on a run, going around stunned people, startled Peyti, and frighteningly calm Disty, sprinting past vehicles that were landing on top of other vehicles and rubble from buildings that hadn't been built to code.

It took forever, but really only a minute or two, to reach the station. It at least was intact. Train doors were open in the passenger sections, but Deshin didn't go into them.

Instead, he ran to the front of the bullet train. Pounding on the door, sending codes he shouldn't have known, codes he had saved from his work with Kerman, and the control room doors eased open.

Deshin jumped inside, Jakande jumping after him, the woman (God, he'd forgotten her name) joining them, but no other team members in sight.

Too damn bad.

Deshin closed the doors, overrode the security protocols, praying that this train was like older bullet trains, because he hadn't done anything like this in twenty-five years.

He was actually hijacking a train.

He had to get out of this city, and waiting for the authorities wasn't going to work.

For all he knew, the authorities were dead.

You can't go through the dome, Jakande sent. *It sectioned here too.*

Dome emergency exit codes are all the same, Deshin sent back. At least they were on the Moon. It was a failsafe, mostly for dome workers, so that they could escape if something went wrong.

Deshin had learned that when he started working in dome maintenance, and he always kept the updated codes in a personal, easily accessible file, even after he left, when the codes came to him as part of the construction files he got through his various legitimate businesses.

Make sure the doors are closing, he sent to Jakande. *Look—with your eyes not your links to make sure we don't kill anyone as we start up.*

Deshin flung every emergency code he had at the dome, putting them on a loop, figuring one of them would open this section and let them outside onto the Moonscape.

If someone was blowing up the domes, he had to get out of them. He had to head home, and he had to protect his family.

With Soseki dead, no one would figure out how to protect Armstrong's dome.

The only thing Deshin could hope for was that these bombs were either on a timer or they were being planted at different times in different places, maybe starting with the cities farthest from Armstrong and working their way back to the port.

He didn't know, he didn't want to ask—not that there was anyone to ask—and he didn't want to worry Gerda or Paavo.

He sent her a message now, hoping it would reach her when the links got re-established: *Heading home, love. We're safe here*, lying through his damn teeth (his damn links) but he didn't know how else to do it, and he didn't want her to panic.

He wanted her and Paavo out of Armstrong's dome, but he wasn't sure if they'd be safe traveling without him. If they got caught in a dome section, they'd be split in half, like his team had been. And he knew that his home, and the school, weren't anywhere near the government sections of Armstrong.

Because that was what blew up here. The section that exploded was near Yutu City's local government buildings, might even have been in them, he wasn't sure, and he wasn't paying attention.

With Soseki dead, the governor-general dying, an explosion in Yutu City, he had to figure that someone was attacking any government building possible.

He didn't confirm any of that. He needed to focus—and he already was.

Somehow, as he started working the train, he had shut off his visual links. He'd done this in the past, his subconscious mind working at minimizing distractions so his conscious mind could work unimpeded.

He managed to get the train started. He programmed in the speed, making sure that the train scanned the route ahead for debris.

Trains like this were built to plow through small debris, but they couldn't handle large things, like parts of buildings and entire pieces of dome.

The route he programmed took the train around the largest domes, just in case they blew up, kept the train in the non-domed parts of the

Moon, the industrial and mining regions, away from any government areas.

Deshin knew he could go faster that way.

And he would be home within the hour, so that he could rescue his family and figure out what the hell to do next.

8

TORKILD PULLED HER TOWARD WHAT APPEARED TO BE A SOLID WALL, covered in screens. Berhane couldn't see them clearly—there were too many other people in the way—but she saw the movement on them.

Torkild, taller than she was, pushed his way through the crowd, his fingers pinching her elbow as he pulled her forward. She stumbled behind him, occasionally banging into someone, usually a short little Disty scurrying to somewhere else.

But sometimes Berhane hit the back of a person bent over a screen or subvocalizing on their links. More than once, she passed someone (often a human male) shouting as if he were alone, "I'm stuck here. Don't you get it? They're not letting anyone in or *out...*"

The cacophony was huge, ear-splitting, and it was giving her a headache. She heard more languages in this drag from one part of the gigantic terminal to the other than she had heard since college.

A group of Peyti stood silently near a clump of chairs and watched. She had no idea if the Peyti were communicating on their links or just thinking that the humans were being stupidly emotional all over again. And she couldn't really tell if they were talking to each other—those masks covered their mouths.

Torkild looked over his shoulder at her, as if she were the one holding them up. He pulled harder, and she emerged through a cluster of people into an open area.

Here, everyone was staring up at the screens. She couldn't help herself; she looked up too.

And wished she hadn't.

She saw Nelia Byler, the governor-general's assistant, clutching a gurney. The person on the gurney had black hair and a grayish face (like Arek?) but Berhane couldn't quite tell who it was.

She turned on her links—all of them—then wished she hadn't. The chatter in them made her feel like her head was full.

She filtered them down to news updates, heard

…attack on Governor-General Alfreda as well…

…going on in Armstrong today? Clearly, these attacks were coordinated…

…uncertain how many other leaders, if any, have been threatened…

She looked up at Torkild.

He had stopped moving, his hand still holding her elbow, but not pinching anymore. His face was squinched. He was looking at her with sympathy, and the look didn't fit on his skin very well. It never had.

"Did you reach him?" Torkild asked.

She hadn't even tried, not since they'd started their mad dash across the crowded terminal.

"No," she said. "But he hasn't answered me."

"I'm sure they have the site locked down," Torkild said.

"But link communications?" she asked.

"I'd be shutting down everything but the emergency links," he said in his lawyer voice. "You don't want rumors to start and you don't want the wrong information to slip out."

Like the fact that everyone else who attended the governor-general's speech might be dead.

Her stomach clenched.

Her father couldn't be dead, he just couldn't. The cruel irony of dying on Anniversary Day aside, he wasn't the kind of man who just died. Not even in a situation like this.

"Come on," Torkild said, and his grip on her tightened.

She couldn't tell if he was disgusted with her. She hadn't answered him, she hadn't even tried to answer him, she just looked up at him like a dazed child, the way she had done when her mother had died and he had shown up at the house. Dazed, terrified—not at all the same woman who had led a train car full of people onto the unstable platform near the bombed-out section of Armstrong.

Torkild walked directly toward the screens, and Berhane tried to pull back. Didn't he see where he was going?

He slipped behind one of the full-sized screens, touched the wall, and a door she hadn't seen before opened. As it did, a sign flashed across her vision:

Earth Alliance Lounge. No Admittance Without Clearance.

She stopped, and pulled him back.

He turned, a frown on his face, then nodded. "It's okay," he said. "I have clearance."

Lucky him.

He led her inside.

The lounge smelled of oranges and wet feet. The weird stench made her eyes water.

The door closed behind her, and as it did, she realized that this room, while smaller than the main luxury terminal, was still quite large. It was filled with dozens of people she recognized—big-shot lawyers, diplomats, and some lower level government officials.

Some were talking to each other, but most were slightly hunched, clearly communicating on their links. A handful watched the screens ringing the room.

Images on those cross-cut between the police working on the crime scene outside O'Malley's, a still shot of Arek's strangely stonelike visage, and that panicked shot of Nelia Byler, clutching a gurney.

Several Disty sat cross-legged on top of tiny tables. There were even more Peyti in this lounge than there had been in the main terminal. These Peyti all sat at tables and tapped on devices held in their sticklike hands. They at least seemed familiar.

Because some of the other aliens didn't.

She wasn't sure she had ever been this close to a group of Rev. They were unbelievably huge, pear-shaped, and had more arms than she could easily see. She'd read some history of the Rev, of them using their size and extra limbs to intimidate humans, and she finally understood it.

The smell near the door came from the cluster of Lynisians near the door. They reeked of oranges, something they ate in large measure (and used as cologne) whenever they came to human-based communities. Oranges weren't available on Lynae.

Most humans kept a big distance from the Lynisians, partly because they were loud, but also because their appearance was uncomfortably strange. They had tentacles poking out of the top of their torsos, like long, out-of-control hair, but at the end of the tentacles, they had hands.

Two long limbs on either side of their torsos ended in faces, which made them very hard to look at. Often one of the limbs would be upside down by human standards, talking to a compatriot's face that was in the same position.

She had had a class with a Lynisian, and he'd required three chairs so that he could lift his faces upright to watch class interactions.

She hadn't been able to look at him then, and she couldn't look at this group now.

Torkild had let go of her arm. He was marching forward to a group of empty, plush, blue chairs in the center of the room.

She stopped following. It was quieter in here, if stranger.

She ran a hand over her face.

Daddy, she sent through her links. *Please answer me the moment you get this. Please.*

She wondered if she should let her brother know that their father was in the middle of this mess. But Bert was on the Frontier, and he probably didn't even know there *was* a mess.

Torkild was shouting at someone—shouting! A man looked up, as if he had done something wrong, and Torkild headed toward him.

Berhane was done traipsing along like the dutiful fiancée. She had thought she was supposed to be talking to Torkild. Instead, he was heading toward someone named Barry who apparently was an old friend.

Berhane leaned on one of the chairs. It slid, which she didn't expect. Most of the furniture in the port was bolted down, but apparently not in here.

Daddy, she sent again. She had a feeling she wouldn't hear from him for some time, but she couldn't stop herself from pinging his links. Maybe she should try his business offices and see if they could track him down.

She might not be on his emergency list, a thought that would once of have twisted her stomach but now seemed as normal as breathing.

She slid the chair back into position. She was suddenly tired and in need of a seat. Maybe she would just close her eyes for a few minutes, and when she did, this long and terrible morning would be over.

She was reaching for the chair when the floor shook. The chair skittered away from her—*bounced* away from her—and she was having trouble staying on her feet.

A couple of the Disty fell off their tables. Two of the Peyti's chairs toppled sideways. The Rev's weird arms came out and caught the walls.

The shaking seemed to go on forever, but she knew it only lasted a few seconds.

People were screaming and shouting. A number of them had fallen, but she hadn't.

She'd been through worse.

She even knew what this was.

The dome had sectioned. For the third time in her life, the dome had sectioned.

She wrapped her arms around her torso and looked up at the screens.

All the images of the governor-general and Arek were gone, replaced by images of burned-out buildings and smoke rising out of the center of domes. Only the areas didn't look familiar. When the bomb had exploded four years ago, that area had still looked like itself. Like a horrible disgusting terrible rendering of a once-lovely place.

She didn't recognize these places.

Voices around her, still shouting, were talking about the sectioning, but she didn't care.

She was looking at those images.

Was she looking at Littrow? Or somewhere else? She thought she saw smoke rising out of one of the craters—Tycho Crater? Damn the Moonscape. It was impossible to tell exactly where the images were coming from.

She was spinning, slowly, staring at the screens, trying to make sense of them, and knowing, deep down, exactly what they were showing her.

The Moon. All of it. Looking like that little section of Armstrong had not four years ago.

The entire Moon.

Torkild reached her side. He grabbed for her, but she didn't let him touch her. He looked panicked.

She didn't need someone who panicked.

Not right now.

Still, her gaze met his.

"Do you know what this means?" she asked—softly, she thought, but with all the chatter, she probably hadn't spoken softly at all.

He shook his head. All the color had leached from his skin. He still didn't look like Arek, though. No one looked like those images of Arek.

"Nothing is going to be the same," she said. "Nothing is ever going to be the same again."

ONE WEEK LATER

9

For days afterward, most everyone went outside after dark and stared up at the sky. The moon was full, or near full, and some of the destruction was visible to the naked eye.

Pippa Landau had been to the Moon more times than she wanted to think about, usually to Armstrong, which was mostly spared. But she had lived on Earth long enough to adopt some of Earth's customs. Or maybe some of the customs of where she lived, a place that proudly called itself the Midwest, even though it was in the middle of no part of the west as she knew it, a place that liked its old names even better, even though the regions it referred to had less meaning than they historically did.

She lived in Iowa.

For a while she had lived near the flat farmland in the center of the region, but she had moved to the bluffs near the Mississippi River after her second son was born. She hadn't thought of those farmlands until the night she learned about what the media was now calling Anniversary Day.

In those farmlands, the darkness would be richer, and the Moon even brighter.

But here in Davenport, right after Anniversary Day, the residents had started turning off lights at dusk, even the automated ones. Everyone gathered in the historic Prospect Terrace Park overlooking the river, where some major treaty, now completely unimportant, had been signed long ago, and she found herself part of "everyone."

She hadn't been to Prospect Terrace Park in more than a decade, and not at night since her children were little and wanted to attend the July summer fireworks party that had continued for centuries, unbroken, from a barge on the Mississippi.

The Anniversary Day gatherings didn't have the festive feel of the fireworks parties or even the annual park blues festival, held in September just before the weather changed.

In fact, she had never in her life experienced anything like these gatherings. She had come to the park on a whim. Her backyard was small and not set up for stargazing. Usually, she didn't look up at night at all. She didn't like to think about what was out there in the known universe, the things that could come for her—and hadn't so far.

So, when she heard about Anniversary Day, she thought about the best place to look at the night sky, and decided on the least developed park, the one that some historical society deemed too important for "services." There were bathrooms at the end of the road, near the very controversial parking lot, but nothing more except benches that were replaced every decade or so as they wore out.

When she drove up the first night after the bombings, she was surprised to see that dozens of others had the same idea. Human, Peyti, Disty—it didn't seem to matter. People from all species had gathered and were looking up, some with real telescopes and some using the scoping feature in their eyes.

She hadn't even thought of a scope. Her eldest son Takumi would have brought one—something high tech and modern. He probably would have been able to see the recovery effort that was going on in all of the ruined domes, down to the broken bits of buildings.

But she hadn't spoken to him or her other children, not since the day after Anniversary Day. All of her children—grown now—lived on Earth, for which she was very grateful. They had their own lives and their own careers, and if they needed her, they would contact her on their links.

She had raised them to be self-sufficient, and they had become so, but they didn't ignore her either. Right now, they were probably dealing with the fallout from the Moon's disaster in their various businesses, not to mention dealing with the friends they might have lost in all of the bombings.

No one outside of Earth seemed to realize just how close Earth and the Moon really were. Their cultures were linked, primarily because the Moon operated as the gateway into Earth itself.

Still, she had learned that the Moon, as perceived by the people on Earth, was more than a gateway, more than yet another civilized place. The Moon controlled the tides. It had an ancient mythical component. Her youngest daughter Toshie had studied the Moon extensively for years, and loved the ancient portraits of the uninhabited Moon as seen from Earth. Toshie particularly loved the purported Man in the Moon.

It had taken Pippa months to see the image that the ancients believed resembled a face. The Moon she knew looked nothing like that. She could see the domes, glinting in the reflected sunlight, looking like pockmarks on the Moon's whitish grayness. She sometimes imagined that she could see all of the activity around the Moon from Earth, even when she couldn't.

But she tried not to think of the Moon or anywhere else outside of Earth. Hell, outside of Iowa, or even Davenport. She had taken a teaching position at a local high school decades ago, and she continued it even now, nurturing the young minds, preparing them for a long life in a complicated universe.

Davenport was exactly the right size for her. She had disliked the small farm communities—they had been too small, and everyone had known everyone else's business—but she liked this medium-sized city, with its humid, continental climate. She loved a climate, period. She had grown up on starbases at the far end of the Alliance, something she never talked about, and had lived in a controlled environment until she was twenty-six years old.

Varied weather—from the deep cold of the plains winter to the hot humid summer—had come as a surprise to her, and had taken her years to adjust to. Now she loved it.

Even on this night, she loved it. The smell of freshly cut grass, the faint scent of roses, the muddy wet odor of the Mississippi herself, gave the park a fragrance all its own. She'd recognized that fragrance as Davenport summer evening, and it comforted her.

Just being outside comforted her. The air was warm and humid, the sounds of the river lapping against its banks soft and gentle. There were no ships on the river that she could see—they were probably docked or anchored for the evening.

And the lights were off, even here, which she had not expected. Nor had she expected the crowd, all looking up, all silent. No one spoke. No one greeted her—unusual in this community, even if no one knew her.

It was as if everyone wanted to be alone and yet together with this inexplicable disaster.

They could have watched it unfold on the nets. They probably were. She knew her second oldest son Tenkou would have had several windows open in his vision even as he stared at the Moon itself. He had always processed more information at one time than anyone else she had ever met.

She hated that practice of his. She had received a hard-fought lesson when she was his age that silence and focus saved more lives than any information ever could. She had learned that her intuition was as important as the facts she had gleaned over time.

Her intuition had brought her here.

Pippa found a spot near a young elm tree. She was certain this area was empty because the others probably believed the small copse of trees would interfere with their view.

She was tiny. Other people would interfere with her view as much as any tree would.

For a moment she was tempted to climb it, but signs appeared in her vision as she looked at it, warning her that the elm had been specially grown from an ancient, nearly extinct stock, and was an experiment, and would she please allow it to live undisturbed?

Any other place would tell her not to climb the damn thing, rather than plead for its continued peaceful coexistence.

She loved that sideways attitude she found in the Midwest. It tried—politely—to convince her that its rules were her ideas.

And it worked. Instead of climbing the tree, she stood as close to it as she could before she looked up.

The Moon seemed larger than usual, or maybe that was just because she was focused on it. The Moon was larger in all of the Earth's imagination at the moment, or maybe in all of the Alliance's. Everyone was thinking about the Moon.

She looked at it unfiltered at first, and saw small black spots she knew she had never seen before. It looked different, darker and grimmer. She wasn't certain if that was because she knew about all the bombs that had gone off, all the destruction and panic that were still continuing, all the lives ended, the lives disrupted, the change thrust upon an entire place, something that would never ever be the same again.

She was glad her children were grown and her husband had passed away. She needed to see this alone.

She took a deep breath of the fresh air, felt the wind blow softly over her, and closed her eyes for just a moment. Then she squared her shoulders, raised her face to the sky, and opened her eyes.

Without thinking about it too much, she telescoped her vision, centering in on one of the dark patches.

It took a moment for the images to coalesce. She saw vast expanses of Moon landscape, and then she saw tiny buildings near what appeared to be a road. Finally, she looked at the darkest area, and gasped.

A dome—she didn't know which one—broken and dark, its jagged edges visible even from this distance. She thought she saw smoke rising from it, but she knew that wasn't possible. Was it dust, escaping from the opening? Dust or ash or something else?

Or was she imagining it, based on all the news coverage she had been trying to ignore?

Her stomach turned, but she made herself look. She looked at the other domes, not quite in the center of her vision. They weren't as round and smooth as they had been. They appeared broken. Or maybe that was how her mind interpreted the data.

Because she could see lights around center pools of darkness, darkness where there hadn't been any before.

She stared at the Moon for the longest time, shuddering, thinking about debris fields and the force that exploded materials exerted as they spiraled outward, away from the explosion.

Even in zero-G.

She closed her eyes, felt her eyelashes, wet and spikey, against her cheek.

"Mrs. Landau?" The voice speaking to her seemed faint and far away. "Mrs. Landau, are you okay?"

She made herself open her eyes. Her cheeks and chin were wet. She blinked, shutting off the telescope, and looked at the sound of the voice.

One of her students. A boy, his face half in shadow. She couldn't think of his name at the moment, which spoke to the depth of her distress. Because she had always been good with names.

Always.

She swallowed so that her throat was lubricated before she tried to speak. "I'm all right," she said. "Thank you."

He didn't move. He was peering at her. She knew who he was; his name just wasn't coming to her. He was the boy who, at the start of the school year, had asked her why she insisted on being called "Mrs." when none of the other married female teachers did.

It's an old-fashioned honorific, she had said, lying a bit. *I like the sense of history.*

He hadn't understood it then, and she doubted he would understand it now. She did like the sense of history, but not the history of the title. The history it spoke of with her husband, a man who had loved her in spite of everything. They had been happy together. They had spent years raising children and being traditional and learning how to live in an old-fashioned world when the rest of the universe seemed to thrive on the edges, on the new.

She had loved that, and even though it was gone, even though she was the only one of her family remaining in Davenport, she wanted to honor it.

"You don't look all right," the boy said after a moment.

"It's just disturbing, that's all," she said, as if destroyed cities were a small thing. "Have you ever been to the Moon?"

He shook his head. "My dad wanted us to come out and look. For the history, you know. He said you'll never forget this."

"He's right," she said softly, then looked up. "None of us ever will."

10

DESHIN SAT AT THE DESK IN HIS OFFICE, SURROUNDED BY SCREENS. He felt like his son Paavo, trying to solve a particularly difficult math problem.

Not that Paavo would have needed a ring of screens to see everything. That boy could see numbers in his mind's eye.

Deshin envied that. He envied his boy's brilliance, and he reveled in it as well.

He shut the screens down for a moment, feeling overloaded, then pushed his chair back. He stood, but kept his back to the wall.

Ever since Anniversary Day, he had felt vulnerable in his office. He had arrived home to Armstrong to find his wife and child worried, but in good health. His city was fine as well, thanks to quick thinking by that security chief, Noelle DeRicci.

In fact, some believed—and he was one of them—that DeRicci had saved millions of lives by ordering the domes all over the Moon to section. Some whack jobs were starting to complain that her order was illegal. It was, but who the hell cared? She took action.

She saved *lives*.

Hell, she had saved *his* life.

He shuddered when he thought about that. He had stepped outside that building, looked up, and in an instant, he would have been dust and molecules, floating because of the Moon's lighter gravity. He would have vaporized, just like his two staff members had.

Just like thousands of his employees had. Employees, friends, people he knew.

The loss he'd suffered—his businesses had suffered—was staggering.

And every day, he thought about how it all could have been worse.

It wasn't like him to dwell on anything bad, and he'd been through a lot of bad in his life. But he'd never been through anything like this.

Hell, the Moon had never been through anything like this—not in its entire history.

Some cultures went through this kind of devastation, but usually as a prelude to some war. He'd studied it in school and promptly forgot it, like all the useless school information that had come his way.

But Paavo was reminding him every night at dinner.

Deshin had made a point to go home every day, to spend time with his beautiful wife and his precious if inexplicable kid. Paavo, who was usually quiet and living inside his brain more than Deshin sometimes thought healthy, seemed to be trying to deal with the crisis in his own unusual way.

Paavo had been talking—Gerda actually said "discoursing"—on all the history he could find. War, after war, after war, displaced cultures, bombed cities, certainly not something that Deshin wanted a child of seven ("almost eight," Paavo would say defensively) to spend his time thinking about.

But if Deshin could, he'd wrap Paavo in expensive gauze and protect him from the world. The boy had suffered enough, thanks to his biological parents (the flaming assholes), and then, after that got settled, this happens.

At least Deshin got to play the conquering hero for his boy. He had gotten the train back to Armstrong in time to pick up Paavo and take him home, reassuring him that all would be fine.

Deshin hated lying to his child.

Nothing was going to be fine. And aspects of all of this bothered him more than he could say.

The math didn't work. Which was what he'd been staring at for the past hour now.

The math bothered the hell out of him, and when something bothered him, he needed to pace.

He collapsed some of the screens and stepped into the main part of his office.

He'd seen this building, this office, as the jewel in the crown of his empire. Not that it was an empire. It was a confederation of businesses, friends, and enemies. He held it together through his will and his considerable fortune.

Although even the confederation was ragged these days. Everything was ragged, like Armstrong itself. He barely recognized it, although he studied it daily from this office.

The office covered the top of one of Armstrong's few high-rise buildings. It was a gigantic bubble, with 360-degree views of the city. The thick, reinforced nanomaterials were clear, but his architects reassured him that the materials would protect him from pretty much anything someone would try to throw at them. A structural engineer put it differently: she had told Deshin that the clear bubble was stronger than any of the walls in any of the nearby buildings.

He used to see this clear office as a screw-you to anyone who wanted to mess with him. A dare. *Try it*, the office seemed to declare. *You can see me, but you can't touch me.*

He had been younger then, and naïve. He had thought that someone who was after him would go after *him*, would try to kill *him*. He had since learned that vengeance wasn't so simple, and that random events not directed at him or his people could harm him more than an attack on his empire.

Last week had proven that.

The empire spread out below him. The rest of the building housed dozens of businesses, many of them shell corporations, that he owned. His main business, Deshin Enterprises, rented the top six floors of the building, which he owned under a different name through a different corporation.

He used to keep all of the twists and turns of his various businesses in his head. Yes, there were a dozen spreadsheets, some of them actually legitimate, but none of them told the full story.

He needed a spreadsheet that did, now. Ever since Anniversary Day, a part of his brain seemed to be reserved for processing the changes, processing his losses, and processing the emotions he felt behind the ones he was supposed to feel.

He couldn't focus on the business as much as he wanted to. Instead, he found himself focusing on the math.

His reflection moved in the window. At least Armstrong set its dome according to Earth light. He could tell the time, just from the appearance of the dome. It was Dome Daylight, bright enough to be midday. He loved the generated sunlight, even if the yellow of the dome's light was somewhat artificial, and he loved the way it cascaded through his office, over the chairs and the desk and the conference table on the far side of the room.

Those little moments, that appreciation of the light, that was new too. It was as if part of him reveled in being alive.

He wasn't certain how many other people inside the sectioned domes understood just how close they had come to disappearing forever.

Unlike them, though, he knew.

He also knew how much explosive it took to breach twelve domes and damage seven others. Not to mention the explosion that nearly happened here, and didn't because of quick thinking on the part of Armstrong authorities.

That math bothered him. It colored his sleep, what little he'd been getting. Because it wasn't *just* the math that bothered him.

It was the coordination in the attacks.

First, an assassination of an authority figure, followed by the destruction of a dome.

There was no real reason to assassinate the authority figure, not if the dome was going to explode anyway. In fact, it could be argued that the assassinations were what tipped off DeRicci and her cohorts. If the assassinations hadn't happened, the Moon might have become desolate all over again.

He didn't think the masterminds behind this gigantic attack—whoever they might be—considered the assassinations as warnings. He suspected the masterminds had meant the assassinations as symbols. Those masterminds wanted someone—survivors, the Alliance itself maybe, the Earth, he didn't know exactly—to understand that the bombings were directed at authority figures, not just at the domes.

The masterminds had had an agenda, and they had failed at a great deal of it. Not every leader targeted had died—again, thanks to the security chief—and not every dome targeted had had a hole blown through it.

For some groups, those failures might have been enough to stop them. For this group—which had clearly spent years planning the attacks—those failures might cause them to regroup and try again.

He paced the length of the office, in the middle of it, avoiding chairs and occasional tables, and found bits of art that Paavo had made during his various years in school. The path he took was a surprising obstacle course; he never walked this way.

In the past, he had always paced around the windows, probably subconsciously daring someone to test the strength of those nanomaterials. He probably should do so again. It wasn't like him to shy away from anything.

Of course, it wasn't like him to be careless either.

He ran a hand through his hair.

There would be a second attack. Someone (or someones) didn't plan that hard to give up at the very first failure. They would try again.

A lot depended on whether or not they had planned on failing in the first place.

If they hadn't planned on failing, the second attack would take longer.

If they had planned on failing—or not entirely succeeding—then the second attack could happen tomorrow.

His stomach clenched and he returned to the seat in front of his desk.

Right now, the authorities were concentrating on search and recovery efforts. They had to put the domes together, they had to figure out who was dead and who was missing and who took the opportunity presented to attempt to disappear.

They didn't have time to trace the attackers.

He did.

He needed to, or he needed to move his family and his businesses off the Moon.

He had already calculated the cost of that. Even though he had billions tied up in corporations that did business elsewhere, the bulk of his business was Moon-based. He'd always been a local guy, and he was paying for it now.

It would cost five years' earnings to move his businesses permanently off-Moon, and that didn't count what would happen to the stock prices of the legitimate businesses. Would the markets see his decision to leave the Moon as prudent or as unwise? If they saw it as unwise, the stock price of his legitimate businesses could plummet even more.

The more money he lost, the more he would have to rely on his illegitimate businesses. He'd been trying to legitimize those since he and Gerda had adopted Paavo. He wanted his boy to inherit an empire he could be proud of, not one that he would need street and survival skills to run.

Paavo didn't have those skills, and if Deshin had his way, Paavo would never gain them—not in a life filled with crisis, the way that Deshin's had been. He wanted Paavo to be one of those dilettante owners, and he wanted to protect the boy from insider theft as much as possible. So when the time came, he would teach Paavo to understand the business, how to run the business, and then how to keep a distant eye on the folks who managed it from day to day.

Deshin couldn't do any of that if Deshin Enterprises had much of its capital in businesses that weren't always legal.

Which trapped him—and his family—on the Moon.

He could shut everything down. He had more than enough money to live on. But the very idea of that gave him the shudders.

As he saw it, there was only one realistic thing that he could do.

He could figure out who was trying to destroy his home and destroy the bastards first.

He had the resources.

He had the investigators.

He had the will.

And best of all, the masterminds—whoever the hell they were—would never see him coming.

11

AVA HUỲNH STARED AT THE INFORMATION SCROLLING ACROSS HER SCREENS. Then she looked at the 3-D image plastered against the back wall of her office:

Twenty young men, all clones of PierLuigi Frémont, laughing as they stood together inside the Port of Armstrong, three weeks ago now. They had arrived two weeks before the catastrophe called Anniversary Day, and they had done their best to destroy every major city on the Moon.

If it weren't for a security chief in a newly minted government that hadn't even applied for Earth Alliance recognition, those young men would have succeeded.

Huỳnh tucked a strand of purple hair behind her right ear, one of the dozen earrings she wore scratching the skin of her finger. She sucked on the scratch absently as she stared at everything around her.

She was drowning in information and none of it made sense. It poured in from dozens of locations, ancient news, old suppositions, arrest records, and problems from earlier eras.

She desperately wanted to find something that would help the people on the Moon solve this massive crime, and so far, she had found nothing.

She wiped her finger on the skirt of her lavender dress. That morning, she had color-coordinated everything, from her hair to her fingernails to her shoes, to make herself feel like she was in control of *something*. But the clothes, hair, and nails had only left her feeling ridiculous.

And in the cafeteria during lunch, at least two of her colleagues asked her if the purple explosion had occurred in her closet or her bathroom.

Sometimes she thought Earth Alliance Security Headquarters for the Human Division was a lot more like high school than any professional organization she had been a part of.

She sank into her chair and ran a hand over her face. She made herself look away from that image of the twenty clones.

Her office was small, but interesting—or at least she thought so. She had chosen it because of its trapezoidal shape. The entire building was oddly shaped, and she loved that about it. The shape of her office seemed appropriate to her, since no investigation was ever perfectly square, but the investigations that got solved had at least two parallel lines, just like a trapezoid.

She'd tried to explain the correlation of the geometrical shape of her office to the shape of a standard investigation to one of her assistants years ago, but he'd given her a somewhat cross-eyed look and said, *I got into investigation precisely because it* didn't *have math.*

He was wrong. The most successful investigations—particularly human investigations—often involved some forensic accounting as well as some basic arithmetic.

Every investigation she had ever been involved in felt like math to her. Sometimes in the investigation, she solved a relatively easy math problem (two plus two), and sometimes she had to use calculus, and sometimes she had to rely on some alien math equations that made her own eyes cross.

Right now, she felt like someone had dumped a gigantic box of centimeter-sized toy numbers on her and told her to make sure they made some kind of mathematical sense. Almost as if the very problem were hidden from her, and she had no idea what kind of equation she needed or what she really needed to solve.

No, scratch that. She knew what she needed to solve.

The Moon attacks were, at their core, a good old-fashioned whodunit. The problem was that there were lots of dunnits to unravel and lots of whos to be found.

Who created the clones? Who raised and fed them? Who trained them? Who sent them to the Moon?

Who wanted the Moon destroyed?

And why?

Whys were always the hardest puzzles to solve. She'd closed many a case without fully understanding the why of it. The who was always easier, even on this scale.

Still, something about this whole thing—its vastness and coordination—bugged the hell out of her.

Then she slapped a hand on her forehead and muttered, "Alien math," and stumbled her way out of her office.

The Earth Alliance Security Division had its own starbase, with layers and divisions all over the base. It was part of what she always thought of as a spider-like web of bases, surrounding the Earth Alliance Human Division for the First Sector. The outlying bases were all attached to the Human Division base by gigantic travel tunnels.

The entire base system was a maze of tunnels and circles, all attached to that gigantic base in the center. The smaller bases, like the Security Division, somehow managed to spin on their own axes (she didn't understand all of the engineering) so that the views changed all the time.

Sometimes the buildings with windows had a view of the stars beyond and sometimes they viewed the travel tunnels or the underside of the Human Division base.

That was the only feature she didn't like about living here. In the past, she had lived on bases or cities that were planet- or moon-side, and the view from a window always remained the same. It had taken her a year of living in the Security Division to realize that it was the view from her apartment window that was disorienting her, not the actual life on the base.

Once she figured that out, she had asked for a windowless apartment deep inside her building, which had the twin benefits of being larger and cheaper than the windowed apartment. And then she opted to take this office, with its straight line walls and unusual angles.

They comforted her.

And oddly, she needed the comfort while considering this case.

Mostly because it pissed her off.

The very idea that someone would launch such a coordinated attack on the Moon pissed her off.

The fact that it was proving hard to solve pissed her off more.

She headed down the hallway, and up five flights of stairs (walking was good for her; she liked real exercise as opposed to enhanced muscles), then across a "sky bridge," which wasn't in the sky at all. It just connected the Human Investigative Unit with the Joint Investigative Unit for this sector—all within the Security Division itself, so she was still in the smaller base.

(She had once tried to explain the way everything connected here to a new hire, without using images, and he had stopped her after about three sentences. *I'll just use the mapping function in my links*, he'd said. She doubted he ever learned how to find his way around without computerized help. She, on the other hand, could find her way through this base blindfolded and without any working internal technology at all.)

The Joint Unit combined Human and Alien investigations. Each Earth Alliance species had its own investigative unit within the Security Division, and the Joint Unit coordinated everything. It also handled investigations that had no real jurisdiction.

Everyone thought the Moon bombings belonged in the Human Division, but maybe everyone was wrong.

She stepped into the main reception area, green with silver trim, with more 90-degree angles than she liked. Everything was precise here, because one thing the Alliance government had learned was that most species felt calmer in predictable spaces—squares, rectangles, circles.

"Most" being the key word here. And it wasn't always consistent inside a species. Because half the human staff hated the trapezoidal offices. And one woman flatly refused to work in anything that wasn't a perfect rectangle.

Huỳnh hated that kind of difficult.

She was a different kind of difficult. A creative kind.

The android receptionist stood when Huỳnh entered. The thing was bipedal, since many species could relate to a biped, and it had an almost-human face. The face could shift depending on what kind of being entered reception, and it could also shift languages faster than any link-guided human could.

Still, it creeped Huỳnh out. Its bluish/goldish/greenish eyes seemed to judge her. No, that wasn't right. It seemed to look at her like *What do you want this time, troublemaker?*

She flushed. Androids weren't supposed to have the ability to judge. They were simply machines that worked on a higher level than the bots that cleaned the place.

She was paranoid and knew it. Not that paranoid was the right word. Pesty. The investigators here thought she wanted to do joint investigations more than was healthy.

But she always figured it didn't hurt to ask.

She had learned not to ask the receptionist to let her pass. She just walked by as if she belonged here. If the damn thing wanted to stop her, it could.

Behind the door, the offices were a Disty-warren of clutter and low ceilings. The design was no coincidence. The first head of the Joint Unit had been Disty, until he was dismissed because he funneled too much information to the Disty government.

A lot of joint security investigations in those dark days had ended in Disty Vengeance Killings before that head had been replaced.

There had been nearly two dozen heads since then, from all different species. The current head was a fussy Peyti male named Xyven. He had one of the highest closure rates the investigative department had ever seen, first in the Peyti Investigative Unit, and then in the Joint Human/Alien Unit. But Huỳnh always felt his management skills left something to be desired.

She grabbed an environmental suit from the rack just inside the Unit. She never brought her own to work, probably because she never thought she'd need it.

Contrary to what some of her colleagues thought, she didn't come to work every day thinking that she would head into the Joint Unit for a casual chat and an invitation to a joint investigation.

She stepped into the nearest restroom to slip the suit on. She used to put the suits on in the hallway, but she eventually learned that wasn't the brightest idea. She'd had more than one skirt ride up to her shoulders as she tried it.

This time, her clothing stayed in place—but of course, she'd picked a suit of the right size. She hated using the company mask, but she knew they had a coating made of nanocleaners that theoretically removed all traces of the previous wearer.

Sometimes, though, she was just too trusting. Or maybe she really did need to bring her own suit to work.

She slipped out of the restroom and headed down the main corridor to Xyven's office. A divider separated the Peyti part of the unit from the human part. She placed a gloved hand on the divider, and tapped her personal code into the material. She also tilted her head so that it could do a retinal scan.

It took a moment, and she temporarily thought her access was going to be denied.

Then a door in the divider pivoted a few degrees, just wide enough to let her in. She stepped into the tiny bubble that the door created to prevent the atmospheres from mixing.

The door closed and the bubble vanished. She now had to wade through the murk that was a Peyti-normal environment.

Peyla was a relatively bright planet, with good light from a young sun. She never understood why the Peyti preferred their space environment to be dimmer than the human environment. Of course, she never asked either.

Xyven's office was at the end of a long corridor. The Peyti atmosphere was thicker than Earth normal, so she always felt like she was swimming even though the gravity was the same.

The door at the end of the corridor opened, and Xyven stood just inside, his long arms spread from door jamb to door jamb. He was spindly, even for a Peyti, and his thin arms looked more like taut rope than like sticks.

He had a pointed chin and almond shaped eyes. It had taken her years to realize that Peyti whose names began with a Xi sound had different facial features as well. Those features were as subtle as changes in human features—something only those deeply familiar with the species would notice.

She also noticed that his gray skin was tinged blue, a sign of emotional distress.

Again? He sent.

She sighed. He was going to criticize her for asking for another joint investigation as well? Didn't anyone *think* in the Security Division?

I told you to check in at reception, he sent.

Her lips twitched. She almost smiled, but knew better. He hadn't been angry at her about a new possible investigation, but about her usual lack of protocol.

Apparently the android in reception had recognized her, or had had some kind of reaction to her intrusion into the unit. It had probably been flagged to look for her.

Check in so that you can have an underling deal with me? she asked, knowing it sounded bitchy, but not caring.

Xyven's skin turned a darker blue. Her barb had hit. He let his arms drop, and he stepped deeper into the office, not quite inviting her in, but not keeping her out either.

She walked inside as if it were her office, not that it could ever be.

Xyven's office had some human furniture, scaled down to accommodate his slight form. It also had strangely shaped Whetting furniture, with the holes and tubes that accommodated the Whetting's multi-appendage form.

Other things scattered around the room looked like sculpture to Huỳnh, even though Xyven had once told her that everything on the floor was furniture of one kind or another.

He was a collector of alien things. Apparently his home—a penthouse apartment in the Peyti-only building near hers—was filled with curiosities and artifacts from almost every species he'd interacted with.

Xyven seemed to prefer the human furniture, probably because it was similar in style to furniture the Peyti used regularly. He retreated to the tall, narrow chair that he had used on previous visits with her.

I don't have time for a long chat today, he sent. He preferred to use links, even inside his office. More than that, the links he insisted on kept a record of the conversation. He claimed he preferred it, because of the lessons he had learned as an investigator.

Some in the human unit believed he did it to prevent any kind of strife. They thought that knowing they were being recorded would change people's behavior.

Maybe it would change some people's behavior, but it didn't change Huỳnh's.

Have you been following the events on the Moon? She sent him. She hovered near a chair in front of him, but wasn't sure if she could sit down. While this environmental suit didn't make her clothing ride up, it was tight enough to make bending uncomfortable.

You are referring to the Anniversary Day massacres, he sent.

I've never heard them called "massacres," she sent.

Millions have died, including many, many of my people. What else would you call it? He sent.

The media are calling this the Anniversary Day attacks.

He shrugged, his thin little shoulders rising up past his pointed chin. When Peyti made that movement with a mask on, it seemed unnatural. When they did it without their masks, it seemed like an affectation.

The end result is the same, he sent. *Murder on a vast scale.*

Yes, she sent, and decided to sit down anyway, despite the fact it was uncomfortable. She could feel the edge of the chair through the thin material of the suit.

You are handling the investigative oversight? He sent.

I am, she sent. *These attacks are coordinated and they were planned years ago. I'm not finding much in my investigation here, so I'm going to assemble a large team and send a lot of them to aid in the investigations on the Moon.*

Good thinking, he sent. *I'm sure the Moon can use all the help it can get.*

He put his spindly hands on the chair's arms and levered himself up.

It seems that you have the investigation well in hand. I appreciate the update.

She didn't move. *I'm not here to give you an update.*

The blue in his skin, which had been fading, rose again. But he sat down.

I want Peyti, Disty, and other non-human investigators to be part of those teams, she sent. *Only you can authorize that.*

This is not a joint human/alien investigation, he sent, folding his hands over the center of his torso. *This close to Earth, the attacks are a human problem.*

This close to Mars, she countered, *the attacks are a Disty problem.*

He couldn't argue with that; the Disty controlled Mars, just like humans controlled Earth.

He tilted his head sideways, his version of acknowledging her point. His skin had faded to its usual gray.

The Moon is considered a satellite of the Earth, he sent, and something in the tone of the linked message added condescension. Or maybe it was just his wording. *That makes the attacks a human problem, solved by human law, investigated by humans. Besides, the attackers are human.*

Not under Alliance law, she reminded him. Two could play the condescension game. *Clones are not human. They're property.*

Human clones point to a human perpetrator, he sent.

I'm sure that's what the real perpetrators want us to think, she sent. The suit was digging into her thighs and her stomach. It was starting to itch. She had to use incredible self-control not to shift in her chair.

You seem to know who the real perpetrators are, he sent.

No, I don't, she sent, *and an attack this big and this long in the making should be easy to trace. By now, someone should have taken credit for it.*

Don't you believe the credit is in those clones? He sent.

I thought so at first, she sent, *but they're some other kind of message, one I don't entirely understand yet. Oh, and by the way, in case you haven't been following this closely, they're clones of a serial killer, which makes them illegal. They might've been made in the Alliance, but only by some kind of criminal company. I'm voting for something outside of the Alliance. So our investigation is going to have to span the Alliance anyway. Why not make it easier, and bring in every species that lost more than one hundred members in the attacks?*

Because that's not how joint investigations originate, and you know it, he snapped.

I know that joint investigations happen when you approve them, she sent.

And I see no reason to believe that non-human investigators will add to our understanding of these massacres. The loss of life of all species is tragic, but it is clear to me and clear to anyone who studies the footage of that day that these attacks were focused at the Moon, a human-centric Earth satellite. Which keeps these investigations squarely in your department and not part of mine.

It had been a long shot. She knew that, and she still felt disappointed that he said no. Worse, she felt disappointed that he wouldn't concede her point: that there was no way to know who or what had authorized the attacks.

Have you thought about how huge this is? she sent. *How deep inside the Alliance it is? How much planning went into it, and how close these attackers came to destroying the Moon? I think it was just luck that they didn't.*

I think you have too many preconceptions, he sent. *Make certain the investigators you send into the field have none.*

She stood, shaking a little, not from the cut-off blood flow due to the suit's tightness, but due to a fury she was having trouble containing. She hated the way that Xyven refused to consider most joint investigations.

It was as if he saw his job as preventing investigations instead of authorizing them.

I was trying to make certain that the investigators I sent into the field had no preconceptions, she sent. *But you just guaranteed that they'll con-*

duct a human-only investigation. And that means that if the perpetrators, whoever they are, used famous DNA to create those human clones to throw us off some non-human motive, they've succeeded.

You're reaching, he sent.

I'm trying to be thorough, she sent. What's your excuse?

His mouth opened slightly. Apparently he wasn't used to anyone talking to him like that, particularly since the conversations were always recorded.

If I were your boss, he started.

You wouldn't be, she interrupted. You're too rigid.

What would you do? His skin was bright blue now. Quit?

Petition for your removal, she snapped. It's easier when you're a subordinate. Unfortunately, I'd have a tougher time with you as it is, since we're in different departments. But I think your lack of vision will bite you on the ass at some point.

Colorful, he sent, apparently not noticing the irony. She hadn't ever seen him that vivid a blue. But irrelevant. I have closed more cases than you.

And I've managed more investigators than you, she sent. I actually believe my staff can do the jobs they're assigned. I don't go out of my way to ensure that they have nothing to do. I send my people into the field.

Wasting resources and costing the division money, he sent.

Solving crime and finding perpetrators, she sent. And I'll do it here, with or without your help.

Without, he sent. Definitely without.

She shot him a look filled with all the fury she'd been trying to suppress. Bastard. Did he just not care about the fact that millions had died? That the Earth Alliance had suffered a serious blow? That this kind of planning wasn't just a one-time thing?

Was he all about his job?

Or did he truly believe that what happened to humans didn't matter to Peyti?

She didn't know, and she wasn't going to waste time finding out.

She needed to get her all-human teams on the ground. She needed to do some planning.

Without him.

Or the Joint Unit's resources.

Still, she'd be offering the damaged governments of the Moon the kind of assistance they needed. And maybe, just maybe, she'd protect the Alliance against further attacks.

Whether they were caused by humans or not.

12

FRAGMENTED DREAMS OF HER MOTHER HAUNTED HER. WHENEVER BERHANE closed her eyes, she saw not the images of disaster that filled the screens and poured across the public networks, but her mother's black hair, with its reddish highlights catching the fake sunlight of Dome Dawn that last morning, the smell of cinnamon coffee in the air.

The sky was red with early morning light, the shopping district illuminated in copper, everything sharp and clear and focused.

Berhane would wake up without feeling rested, pressure in her chest from unshed tears. Those months after the bombing, those months when she kept hoping and hoping and hoping that her mother had somehow gotten away, that she had survived and lost her memory, that—ridiculously—she had decided to run away from home and not tell anyone, that she was still breathing somewhere. The "magical thinking," as her father called it, had trapped Berhane as surely as the sectioned dome had trapped those inside it for just an instant, before their world evaporated into nothingness.

Then Berhane learned the sequence, realized the bomb had gone off first and the dome had sectioned afterwards, that everyone was dead before Berhane had even known anything was wrong, that her mother hadn't been trapped, but had walked blithely toward the Shenandoah Café, thinking the morning beautiful and soon she would be talking with her very annoyed daughter.

Annoyed.

Berhane still felt the guilt of that.

She could only handle two or three of those dreams per night. She would get up afterwards, and usually get some coffee or a muffin and sit on her balcony on the dome side of her father's house. She had moved back in after Anniversary Day because her apartment had too much Torkild in it.

He had helped her pick out the furniture, had slept in that bed on the final morning of their engagement, had betrayed her there. She was subletting the place to a friend, but Berhane knew she wouldn't return.

Besides, she liked to think that this way Torkild couldn't find her.

Or maybe he would be too embarrassed to come here.

He was on the Moon still—everyone was; no private ships had left yet—and he had only tried to contact her once since that awful day. She had told him she didn't want to think about him anymore, and had shut down all of his access to her links.

To escape him, and all thought of him, she had moved into the suite of rooms that her mother had remodeled for guests. Berhane's childhood bedroom remained, but Berhane wanted to leave that as it was—a monument to a person who no longer existed.

Besides, if she stayed in the suite, she felt like a guest in her father's home instead of a little girl moving back for comfort. She was already looking for a new place, one that wasn't as upscale as Torkild liked, one that had a bit of attitude, maybe even a funky groove, one that didn't show off her wealth, but showed off her personality instead.

Her father's house did show off his wealth. He owned a disgusting amount of land at the northern edge of Armstrong. The area had been settled forty years ago, the dome expanded to accommodate, and covenants added so that no one could build a new subdivision on the empty Moonscape beyond.

The covenants had been no big deal, mostly because there were small craters and hills on this part of the Moonscape. If someone wanted to build there, they would have to make the subdivision a "natural" one, incorporating all of the natural landscape—something more expensive than it seemed since Moon dust was always a problem inside the domes.

Her favorite feature of her father's house was the balcony view of the Moonscape. Blasted and barren, with only small signs of civilization across it. The tracks from whatever had driven across the moon dust recently, a few of the Growing Pits to the east, the high-speed train to Littrow to the west.

If the dome settings were just right, she could see the white-and-blue blur of the high-speed train, the lights of Littrow in the distance, glowing across the black-and-gray Moon. And she remembered, whenever she saw that, how much she loved this place, and how terrified she was for it.

Millions had died a week ago. *Millions.* The domes were devastated, community leaders murdered, the violence on a scale that even now she had trouble imagining.

And yet, on the microcosmic scale, she knew what it was like. Four years ago, against her father's wishes and her brother's advice, she had suited up and gone into the bomb site. She had wanted to stand where the Shenandoah Café had been, where that sidewalk that her mother had walked along had been.

The area had been black with soot from the chemical fires that had flared before the oxygen all escaped from the hole in the dome. The sidewalk still existed, twisted and gray from Moon dust. The Shenandoah Café still had its famous counter and the mural behind it, a mural that got salvaged thanks to the efforts of Berhane and the Café owner's family.

She had found so many things—shattered coffee mugs, spoons, a single shoe—but she had never found her mother.

For nearly three years—after the bombing, after the funeral, after everyone else had seemingly put the entire crisis behind them—Berhane would imagine her mother walking through the front door of this house and asking everyone to forgive her. Her imaginary mother would say that she hadn't realized how much time had passed. She had lost her memory, lost herself, but she had found both again, and she was back.

Then they found her DNA, and Berhane had mourned all over again.

Only a year ago.

And now, this.

Berhane stood on the balcony, cupping the coffee she had had sent up from the kitchen, picking at a muffin made with real blueberries from the Growing Pits, and sighed.

She was so tired, and yet she couldn't rest. She needed to do something. She'd been throwing money at every charity she could think of, but hadn't felt like she had done anything.

It actually felt like cheating.

She set the coffee on a nearby table, then went into the bedroom, grabbed a sweatshirt she'd commandeered from her brother's room on the night of Anniversary Day (it was the only way to bring Bert back home, at least for the evening), and slipped on a pair of loose pants.

She left her feet bare.

Then she went back onto the balcony, got her coffee, grabbed a handful of muffin, and headed out of the suite.

Initially, she thought she'd take a tour of the house, just to stretch her legs without going onto the grounds. Sometimes, looking at the Moon-centric art that her father had collected over the decades made her feel better.

But today, she knew it wouldn't.

Instead, she thought maybe she'd cook something. She hadn't done that in more than a week. And cooking focused the mind, even if it was only for a short period of time.

She padded down the front stairs, her feet sinking into the deep, warm carpet. The warm coffee spilled a bit over her hand, and she licked it off.

Voices echoed across the foyer. She frowned, called up the clock inside her right eye, and saw that it was barely eight in the morning. Her father usually started his day at nine, with a heavy breakfast before he made his way to the office. He stayed there until one or two in the morning, rarely making it home to get his normal six hours of sleep.

She crossed the cold marble of the foyer and walked through the formal living area into the formal dining room.

A dozen top executives from her father's company sprawled in the chairs, a breakfast spread of eggs and cereal and fruit on one side, dim sum and some kind of stir-fry on the other, and in the middle, more pastries than she had seen since the wedding brunch for her best friend from Aristotle.

"Daddy?" Berhane asked.

The conversation stopped—not guiltily, just the way conversations did when an outsider showed up.

Her father smiled at her. He looked wide awake and cheerful this morning, his ruddy face clean-shaven, his black eyes twinkling. He was a big man who slouched whenever he sat down, and this morning was no exception. His head was at the same level as everyone else's. If her father sat up all the way, he'd tower over all of them, even as he sat.

"For those of you who don't know," he said to the collected executives, "this is my daughter Berhane. Be nice to her. She will run the company one day."

Murmured hellos, disinterested and somewhat sheepish, rose around the table. Berhane smiled at all of the gathered executives, even though she didn't feel like smiling at all.

"Join us, my girl," her father said, using his personal nickname for her even though he was in a business meeting. "You should probably be part of this."

She didn't want to join any kind of meeting. She took a sip of her coffee as a stall.

"What are you discussing?" She couldn't quite tell from the assembled executives. Sometimes, her father's choice of business partners told her all she needed to know.

"Rubble and rebuilding," her father said cheerfully.

Her stomach clenched and she was sure her dismay showed on her face. But typically, her father didn't seem to notice.

"Show her," he said to the white-haired man beside him. That man was younger than her father. The white hair, which was all one color, was clearly an affectation, not something hereditary.

Berhane started to protest, but before she could get the words out of her mouth, screens appeared all around her. They were covered with before-and-after pictures. Or now-and-future pictures, if she wanted to be more accurate.

Near each executive was a domed Moon city, with its destruction on full display. The hardest to look at was Tycho Crater, whose central dome had imploded along with a resort built at the top of that dome, against any kind of Earth Alliance regulations. The debris there was meters deep and probably housed thousands of bodies.

Next to it, a new version of the resort, Top of the Dome, rose on stilts and wasn't attached to the dome at all, but seemed to be. Little side pods moved even closer to the dome and the top of the crater, all of them marked with some kind of moniker—hotel, restaurant, shop.

Berhane gripped her coffee cup hard so that her hand didn't shake.

"You're working on the rebuild?" she asked, hoping her voice sounded neutral.

"No one's hired us yet," her father said, "but they will when they see how much we've done."

He owned one of the largest construction companies in the solar system. He had built entire subdivisions on some of the moons of Jupiter. He had built the now-destroyed government offices in the center of Littrow. He had built so many things that Berhane couldn't quite keep track of all of them.

And that was just one branch of the corporation she would eventually run. One small arm that, in theory, didn't look at the other arms, which had their fingers in real estate Alliance-wide, in building materials, in demolition, and in so many things that she honestly couldn't keep track.

If her father died tomorrow, she would have to take a small course in the history of the corporation just so that she knew what she was in charge of.

"I don't think anyone's ready to rebuild," she said softly. "Every single destroyed dome section is a crime scene."

"We've handled crime scene restoration and repair," one of the executives said. She didn't recognize him. He was a round little man whose bald head looked deliberately shaved. His coffee-colored pate reflected the overhead light—and not in a good way.

"I'm aware of that," she said in her coldest voice. She could reprimand him. She couldn't reprimand her father. "With this kind of mess, I suspect it'll take months before anyone can even contemplate moving the rubble or rebuilding."

"The domes need covering," another executive said, a woman this time. She had hair as red and fake as the white-haired guy had. "Survivors will need to know that life goes on."

Berhane had to set her coffee cup down on the nearby buffet. If she didn't, the cup would shatter in her hands.

These executives were talking to her like she was like a stupid child, which she was not. She knew her father hadn't told them anything about her, so they were all showing off to her father, trying to impress the boss without calling his intelligence into question.

One way to do that was to show the stupid child what she would be up against when she finally came into the organization.

Those executives weren't the only ones who could play the let's-talk-to-someone-else-while-really-speaking-to-the-boss game. She could too.

"I think you're all being premature," she said. "In case you've forgotten, my father and I have been through this before. My mother died in the Armstrong bombing, the one that everyone considers a precursor to last week's events. Back then as well, dozens of companies pressed the government of Armstrong to hurry and rebuild. Arek Soseki, rest his soul, agreed. And now, it's clear that had he actually allowed the police time to investigate, we might have prevented a Moonwide disaster of unbelievable proportions."

"Berhane," her father said with a bit of reprimand in his own tone, "we're not talking to governments yet. We're just getting prepared."

"It's too soon," she said directly to him.

"Clean-up will begin with or without us," said another man at the far end of the table. "We should be part of it all."

"Because there's a lot of money to be made," Berhane said to him, deliberately keeping her voice neutral.

"Yes," he said.

"Because someone will be making that money," she said, "so it might as well be us."

"Yes," he said, glancing at the others, who were wisely keeping quiet.

"Because we made so much money four years ago," she said in that same tone. "What was it? Millions?"

"More than that," someone else said. "Just on cleanup alone, we charged the city two billion dollars."

"One city, two billion for clean-up of something smaller than what happened in each of nineteen domes." Berhane looked at the rubble images, which, she knew, were there in two-dimensions because that made the images less real.

Her gaze met her father's. He gave her his warning look.

She ignored it.

"So," she said. "Just on clean-up, if we get the bid, we'll make more than 38 billion, probably something closer to 50 billion."

"Our projections show about 100 billion," said a woman at the far end of the table, "and that's if we only get half."

Berhane nodded. "Then we get money for the rebuilding materials from one of our subsidiaries, money for the processing of the rubble for the investigators from another of our subsidiaries, money for recycling and salvaging everything that can be cleaned, money for our architectural firms, money for each building we contract for—am I missing anything? Oh, yes, what my father mentioned from the start. Money for making sure the domes are properly repaired."

"Berhane," her father said warningly. He knew the tone. The rest of them didn't.

"It's been a week," she said to him.

"It's going to get done with or without us," he said. "Last time we came in late—"

"And we still made two billion on clean-up," said the bald guy, obliviously.

"We were late," Berhane said, "because Mother *died* in there, and we were thinking about—"

"Ourselves," her father said. "We don't have to do that this time."

As if it were required to think about the dead, not something that just happened out of love or honor or anything else. As if they had been following a rule, and not their hearts.

Maybe her father had been. Maybe Bert had shielded Berhane from it.

Maybe that was why he left.

She made herself take a deep breath. She wouldn't be able to stop this meeting. Her father would just move it to his office or somewhere else, and wouldn't tell her what happened.

She picked up her coffee cup, no longer afraid she would crush it.

"I'm not dressed to join you," she said. "You all go ahead. I'm sure I'll be brought up to speed at some point."

Then she pivoted on her bare feet and headed back across the foyer.

She finally understood what had happened these past few years. She hadn't been engaged to Torkild. She'd been engaged to a less charming version of her father.

No wonder her mother wanted to warn her.

No wonder Bertram left.

Only Berhane wouldn't leave.

She'd learned a lot of tricks from her father over the years. She already had shares in the corporation. She'd quietly buy up more of them, using some holding companies. She'd amass power without him even realizing it. And she'd exercise that.

But that was the long-term plan.

In the short term, she would do something different. She had been throwing her money at various charities. Now she'd investigate what needed to be done.

Her father's people, his companies, would destroy DNA, ruin any hope that families had of finding if their loved ones died on Anniversary Day.

She'd do her best to stall that destruction. She'd prevent it, and she'd make sure the families got closure.

She just had to figure out how to do it—and do it right.

13

PIPPA ALWAYS LOVED THE FIRST DAY OF SUMMER SESSION. THE DAY WAS invariably sunny. She couldn't remember ever suffering a thunderstorm, even in the afternoon.

The kids would complain, as they had at the beginning of every single summer session of their short lives. Why, they would invariably ask, did anyone have to be inside on a day like this?

And she would always take her students to the garden in the middle of the rectangular building. The garden was large, protected on all sides by red brick that had to be refortified with a nanocoating every year or so, and by mid-June, smelled of half a dozen different flowers, all competing for the most beautiful and the most fragrant.

Because she planned ahead, she always got the outdoor classroom. A covering would slide across the top of it on rainy days, but she would rarely use that. She set up the chairs herself, and used a giant floating screen rather than individual ones to hold the students' attention.

She loved how they would stumble into her "classroom" and smile with delight.

On the first day of summer session, she would arrive an hour before anyone else, primarily for setup, but also to enjoy the garden before the students learned to tame it. She taught biology, and in the summer months, she focused mostly on botany since the school didn't offer any formal classes in that discipline.

She taught inside and outside: the students had to maintain an outdoor garden patch and a small hydroponic garden, so they could learn the difference between a contained garden and an uncontained one. So many of her students would send her thank-you messages after they arrived at whatever college they planned to attend, because they were often the only Earth-based students who had learned how to do indoor gardening as well as outdoor.

It was yet another way that Earth education fell short, at least in her opinion. Education on Earth was always Earth-centric, as if Earth were the *only* place in the universe.

She used to complain that Earthers believed Earth was the center of the universe, and then one of her colleagues pointed out that as far as the Earth Alliance was concerned, Earth *was* the center of the universe.

Pippa stopped making that comparison.

The garden's ground was soft and moist this morning. There had been a heavy dew the night before, and it glistened on the leaves. The earth smelled of loam, a scent she had learned to love.

She stood in the early morning sunshine and thought how perfect the day was, then felt a stab of guilt because she was acutely aware of how much suffering continued on the Moon.

Usually, she ignored all disaster coverage, or she'd drown in it. The Earth Alliance was huge, and there was always something horrible happening somewhere. But the Moon's crisis felt touchable, perhaps because the Moon had remained so visible in the night sky ever since the attacks. She couldn't ignore this one as effectively as she had ignored the other disasters.

At least she had managed to avoid *most* of the coverage.

Not because she was cruel, but because the attacks reminded her of her last year in the Frontier.

She dismissed the thought. She didn't want anything to ruin her day. She wanted to see the surprise on the kids' faces, enjoy the way that her class always became their favorite in the summer, not because they liked her best but because they could indulge in the great outdoors.

Pippa grabbed the small chip that would become the large screen. She often let it float in the early sessions, but today, she'd put it against the windows of the cafeteria. Too many students stared longingly on the first day, before they realized they could transfer into one of her classes, and she wanted to prevent that.

She set up the screen, placing it in the perfect position. Then she flicked it on, to see if she should make the background white or if she could safely make it translucent. It would depend on the light, of course, but also on whatever was going on inside the building behind it.

She rounded the chairs and stood against a pioneer rosebush that had been on this location for centuries, nurtured and cultivated long past its usual lifespan. She loved those white roses and their unbelievable fragrance. She sniffed before she looked up at the screen—

And froze.

Images of twenty men, all identical, laughing as they made their way through a port, scrolled across it, under the heading of Moon Bombers. Her breath caught, her heart pounded, and her knees buckled.

She had collapsed in the dirt before she even realized what had happened.

She didn't need sound to know that those men were clones. She had seen them before—sometimes she saw them in her nightmares. Always, always in a group, but never laughing.

Marching, together, their boots stomping, stomping, stomping in unison, and she was running…

She wiped a hand over her face and made herself take a deep breath. She was imagining this, dreaming it. It couldn't be real.

She hadn't seen that face in more than thirty years. She had watched for it. Her husband had always told her she'd be safe, no matter what, but he hadn't seen them, those blond men who always worked in groups—

But not laughing.

Not once in thirty years had she had a vision of them laughing.

She made herself look up again.

The image on the screen now was of devastation in one of the Moon's domes. Androids and machines working in the rubble, trying to recover something, to clean out the debris. People sitting with each other in hospitals, humans gesticulating as they explained what had happened to them. Rev talking about their experiences.

The things she had tried to ignore every day for more than a week now.

She couldn't stand, not yet. She set up her link to the screen, then commanded it to show the images of the bombers again.

And there it was: twenty men, clones of PierLuigi Frémont—something she hadn't known—entering Armstrong's port fourteen days ahead of the bombings. Going their separate ways.

Clones of one of the most well-known serial killers in human history. She frowned, trying to wrap her brain around that.

Why hadn't she known that?

Why hadn't she known any of this?

She had thought they couldn't get into the Alliance. She had thought she was safe from them.

She bowed her head, hiding it between her knees, the scent of her favorite rosebush overwhelming her.

She felt trapped for the first time in her life. Here, in the center of the Earth Alliance, where she had thought she was safe.

Where she thought she could settle in.

Where she thought she would never ever have to run away again.

14

DESHIN HATED TRAVELING TO CRATER DE GERLACHE. THE CITY DISTURBED him. It was built deep inside the actual crater, with buildings and streets on various levels. He always thought of Crater de Gerlache as a wannabe starbase rather than a domed city on the Moon.

It hadn't even been big enough for the twenty damned clones of PierLuigi Frémont to target. That honor went to Crater de Gerlache's sister city, Sverdrup Crater, whose dome towered over the entire area. Rather than confining itself to the actual crater, the founders of the City of Sverdrup Crater saw the gigantic hole in the ground as the beginning of their city, rather than the thing that contained it.

Until ten days ago, when one of those damned clones blew a hole in the multi-faceted dome, Sverdrup Crater had been one of the prettiest cities on the Moon.

Deshin hadn't even stopped there on his way to Crater de Gerlache. Usually he took a bullet train and spent a few days in Sverdrup before steeling himself for Crater de Gerlache, but this time, he brought his own transportation.

He suspected he would do that for a while, after his Anniversary Day experience.

Still, as his shuttle flew over Sverdrup, he couldn't help but look at the broken edges of the dome. Pieces littered the ground between Sverdrup and the open Shackleton Crater. He would wager some pieces even went into Shackleton, which probably caused energy corporations turmoil. They used Shackleton to collect (and ship) energy from various natural sources—solar energy from Shackleton's rim, and other forms of energy from the cold trap in the eternal darkness of its interior.

He didn't know all the details, only that Shackleton had always been too important to the Moon to inhabit. That was why Sverdrup and Crater de Gerlache were founded in the first place; they had originally housed the workers from two different Earth countries (back when they competed for business centuries ago), and then became domed cities in their own right.

Crater de Gerlache had always been the poor cousin. The perpetual darkness, which Sverdrup fought both by building towering structures over its crater and by brightly illuminating the depths of its crater, seemed to define Crater de Gerlache.

Not only was the crater's interior dark because of the crater's structure, but because the creatures that lived down there really didn't want to interact in the light.

On a bad day, he had once expressed that theory to Gerda, and she had accused him of being poetic.

She had never been to the Moon's south pole. She may have thought he was being poetic, but in reality, he had just been stating a fact. There were people living in Crater de Gerlache who made Luc Deshin uneasy. And it took a lot of work to do that.

He was heading to see one now, a man who lived at the very bottom level of Crater de Gerlache, just above the dome supports, the environmental units, and the structures that maintained the crater's integrity.

Ernest Pietres dealt in small illegal things, from certain kinds of drugs to tiny weapons. If it was tiny and didn't have to be moved with a vehicle, Pietres specialized in it.

If it was larger, then Pietres knew where to find it and who sold it.

Early in his career, Deshin had used Pietres a lot, primarily for information, but not always.

Deshin had confirmed through some back channels that Soseki and the governor-general had been killed with an injection of zoodeh. It took very little zoodeh to kill, just a pinprick's worth.

But zoodeh had been banned in the human parts of the Alliance for decades. The Port of Armstrong actively quarantined any vehicle that brought zoodeh onto the Moon. There was a huge repository of zoodeh in the quarantined ships in the port, but Deshin had a hunch there was even more zoodeh that had been on the Moon, unused, since the ban was instated.

He wanted to confirm that through Pietres.

If anyone knew, Pietres would.

And this was something Deshin couldn't discuss on any link. Traveling here was a risk, but he didn't dare send anyone in his stead, not to ask these questions.

This was the kind of discussion that one old friend had with another, usually in private. Although Deshin couldn't be entirely private: he had brought Keith Jakande with him.

Deshin didn't trust any other members of his security team to accompany him on something this delicate. Jakande had picked a few team members to guard the shuttle, but that was it.

Jakande had been with Deshin long enough to know just how shady Deshin's former business partners were. No one else on the current security team had any idea of the depths Deshin had sunk to—figuratively and literally—as he built his business.

Deshin had brought two weapons with him, not counting whatever Jakande carried. But more important than that, Deshin wore a skintight suit underneath his clothing, which covered all of him except his hands and his face.

He knew that keeping those parts of him uncovered was a risk, but he needed to take that. He doubted anyone, particularly an old business associate like Pietres, would prick him with something laced with zoodeh during a handshake. Zoodeh—even in small amounts—was unstable. Releasing it with a handshake could backfire and kill the perpetrator as easily as it killed the intended victim.

As Deshin got deeper into the lowest level of Crater de Gerlache, he regretted not wearing a full environmental suit with mask.

The air down here had an unclean tang, probably because the environmental systems funneled the freshest air upward. The highest levels of the city housed the major infrastructure, the hotels and restaurants, and the middle class.

The rich—at least those who made their living by honest means and weren't afraid to flaunt their wealth—lived in Sverdrup, one short bullet train ride away.

Deshin hadn't been down here in years. It was as dank and dark as ever. The walls of the lower buildings had moisture beading on them. On some, mold grew, finally telling Deshin what that tang was. It was anti-mold sprays for buildings too old or too cheap to use nanoprotectors. He wished he had brought a mask with him.

His eyes stung, and he sneezed more than once.

We can't stay here long without some kind of facial protection, Jakande sent, always vigilant.

There are decontamination chambers on the upper levels, Deshin sent.

Oh, that'll be fun, Jakande sent, and then the men grinned at each other.

Neither of them wanted to go through a decontamination chamber. But it was the best alternative. Deshin wanted to seem comfortable down here, a task that got harder and harder with each passing step.

They were heading to a small little shop in one of the oldest parts of the lowest level. Deshin knew the shop was still in business; some of his partners still had contact with the shop's owner, Ernest Pietres. Deshin hadn't told Pietres that he was coming; Pietres wasn't the kind of man you ever gave any warning to.

Besides, Deshin had no idea how Pietres felt about him after all these years.

The sidewalks down here were uneven, cracked, and in a few places so broken they were impossible to walk on. Deshin and Jakande had to walk around the broken sections.

Deshin saw no vehicles. The signs that had appeared as Deshin and Jakande descended to this level informed them that flying vehicles were prohibited at this depth. Only vehicles already approved for use on this level would be allowed here.

He also saw very few open and intact businesses. Some of the buildings had disintegrated enough so that he could see the gloom inside. The smell of mold wafted out of a few of them, combining with the chemical stench that seemed to define this level.

At some point, they're going to have to abandon this place, Jakande sent.

Deshin didn't acknowledge that point, primarily because he disagreed. As long as there were intact buildings, someone would do business down here.

The storefront he was heading to was unmarked. He recognized the old-fashioned blue doorknob, and knew better than to touch it. Instead, he splayed his hand over the dirty window, hoping Pietres used the same system he had used in the past.

Deshin still had an ancient chip Pietres had given him, hidden in his lifeline. The chip carried a record of their business dealings and a passcode that, in theory, Pietres' businesses would always recognize.

For a moment, Deshin thought that "always" had ended. Then the door beeped, clicked, and slid open.

He stepped into darkness so absolute his stomach clenched. He couldn't see anything, not even with the light from the street filtering inside.

Stop, Jakande sent. *You're being stupid.*

He grabbed Deshin's arm to pull him out when the lights came up, revealing a slender, red-headed girl standing behind one of the tables. Her skin was an odd butterscotch color—not the kind of pale that some people were, but not as dark as most people either. Her eyes were the color of tap water, so faintly gray as to be almost clear.

She was one of the strangest looking people he had ever seen.

"How do you know this place?" she asked.

"I'm an old friend of Ernest Pietres," Deshin said. "I need to speak to him."

She glanced sideways, apparently at a screen only she could see. "Your code is twenty-five years old," she said, "and I see no record of use after you received it."

"I don't know you," Deshin said. "I need to talk to Ernest. He'll know who I am."

"I know who you are too, Mr. Deshin," the girl said. "I just don't know what you're doing here."

I don't like this, Jakande sent.

Deshin ignored him.

"Well, I don't know who you are," Deshin said to the girl, "so I don't plan to tell you anything. I need to speak to Ernest. Now."

She let out a small laugh and shook her head. "Good luck with that."

"This isn't his business any longer?" Deshin asked.

"You could say that," she said.

"Tell me where to find him then, and I'll leave you alone," Deshin said.

He could feel Jakande a half step too close to him. At least the man wasn't sending him messages at the moment.

"You can't find him," the girl said. "He's dead."

Deshin had opened his mouth to argue with her claim that he couldn't find Pietres, when he realized what else she had said.

"I'm sorry," Deshin said. "I didn't know. Anniversary Day?"

It seemed logical, with so many dead, that Pietres would have been in the wrong place at the wrong time.

She shook her head, casting those strange eyes downward. "The week before."

Deshin's stomach clenched. He heard Jakande release a breath beside him.

"What did he die of?" Deshin asked.

"He didn't 'die of' anything, Mr. Deshin. That implies some kind of disease or natural cause." The girl glared at him. "No. He was murdered."

Murdered. A week before Anniversary Day. "Murdered by whom?"

"You wouldn't believe me if I told you," she said.

"Try me," Deshin said. "These days, I'm in the mood to believe anything."

15

THE OFFICES OF CITY OF ARMSTRONG SEARCH & RESCUE WERE IN ONE OF the giant warehouses just outside the city's dome. The thinking wasn't that S&R needed to be outside the dome for safety's sake; rather S&R put its base out there for the cheap rent and because it needed a lot of space for its equipment.

Moon-based hazards included all kinds of incidents—from dome fires to collapsed mines. Berhane had heard about accidents in the Growing Pits that made her skin crawl, and problems on various spacefaring vessels in orbit around the Moon, which fell into Armstrong's jurisdiction.

All of the search and rescue operations on the Moon were not Alliance based or even through the United Domes of the Moon, which was still such a new government that half the organizations hadn't been set up yet.

Instead, S&R got handled by the community—or not, depending on the community's size and its attitude toward government. Some of the outlying communities like Sverdrup Crater opposed strong government, and now had no real way of handling the crisis caused by the explosion inside their dome.

Because Armstrong hadn't been hit this time, its S&R became the coordinating organization for search and rescue in the various cities. From what Berhane could tell from the media coverage, many Alliance cultures would be sending their own S&R units to the Moon—but they were taking their own sweet time getting here.

She had taken her own sweet time as well. It wasn't until this morning's encounter with her father's executives that she realized she couldn't just sit around the house and wait for something else to happen. She had to take action, and she wasn't sure what that action would be.

She knew what it wouldn't be. She wasn't suited to help hospitalized victims or victims who had lost homes and relatives. She had empathy, in theory, but in practice she had little patience for people who did not know how to help themselves.

After she left that meeting, she sat in her father's kitchen and used his networks to do research on the organizations that were actually doing something outside of Armstrong. She had given money to a number of them, but her conversation with the executives had made her realize that she no longer wanted to just give funds.

She wanted to work.

Check that. She *needed* to work.

Once her research was complete, she put on a pair of old gray pants, a thick work shirt, and some hiking boots from the days when she had believed she could do urban stair climbs to stay in shape. She tied her hair back, pocketed her standard identification and one credit slip, and drove herself to the edge of the dome.

From there, she took public transportation to the warehouses of Armstrong S&R. She had to sign a waiver before getting on the train, because she wasn't wearing or carrying an environmental suit. She'd never taken public transportation outside of the dome before. She had always ridden in an existing protective bubble—one of her dad's vehicles, or some other organization's shuttle.

She hadn't realized that just to go from inside to outside was an adventure in and of itself.

She didn't like to admit how much she hated riding trains. Ever since her mother died, Berhane had done what she could to avoid trains. They made her nervous.

Ironically, when she was forced to take the train, she never thought of her mother. She always thought of that Peyti with the broken arm. He had turned out to be a lawyer named Uzvaan, on his way to give a guest lecture to an Aliens and Alliance law class.

She had tried to stay in touch, but he hadn't wanted her to.

I do not wish to offend, he had said to her at one of the mandatory police interviews with the victims of the bombing, *but I do not wish to socialize with anyone with whom I share tragic memories.*

She had understood the sentiment, but at the same time, she had hoped to find someone who felt as she did about that day. And to her, that meant someone who had gone through the same event.

She hadn't really spoken to anyone else in that train car except the large man, whom she never saw again, so she didn't quite feel the bond of shared experience with the other people she had met at the interviews.

Eventually, she chalked up her interaction with Uzvaan to cultural differences. All he had done, without realizing it of course, was reinforce the negative stereotypes she had about all the different alien species.

Stereotypes she had learned from her father, who had had his problems dealing with aliens throughout the Alliance.

She needed to revise her opinions now, especially the ones she had formed through her father and Torkild. Neither man was an upstanding citizen, and they both had prejudices that she had shared for solidarity's sake, not necessarily because she agreed with them.

It was time that she did things the way she wanted to, not the way her father wanted or her mother had hoped, and not the way Torkild expected. Bertram had moved to the Frontier to get away from the family's influence, but Berhane wasn't going to run.

She loved the Moon, and someone had attacked it. She couldn't find the attacker, but she could help it heal in her own small way.

The train's journey was a strange one. It originated in a station just inside the dome. Even if Berhane had been traveling on another train, she would have had to disembark and go through the station before boarding this one. Inside the station, she had to sign all that documentation filled with warnings. She also had the opportunity to rent an environmental suit (that didn't look exactly clean), just in case the train derailed or someone broke the external seal by trying to exit too soon.

Unlike the bullet trains that crisscrossed the Moon, these old trains to local sites just outside the dome, like the Growing Pits or S&R, did not have android guards or even external safety equipment. The journey was too short and too quick to warrant that kind of expenditure.

Every passenger, then, was on her own. And Berhane was informed that she would be responsible for herself once she left Armstrong's jurisdiction. Only the warehouses themselves were part of Armstrong, but not the land between the dome and the warehouses.

Legally, these areas were unincorporated. Some of them were owned by various entities, but not through the closest city. Squatters' rights still applied to unsettled areas of the Moon.

Berhane's father had filed numerous lawsuits to claim land between the domes. And the farther that land was from bullet train tracks, the easier it was for her father to register his ownership through various means.

She hadn't followed all of it—or really any of it—and she didn't entirely understand it.

After this morning, she decided that maybe she should learn exactly what her father had been doing and why. She had a hunch that she would not approve.

Until she was faced with the short trip across no man's land, she hadn't realized what kind of impact these areas had on the Moon. She had known intellectually that the areas were different, but she hadn't thought about the strain that put on everyday folks.

She knew that a lot of the rules were made by people like her father, who wanted no liability, instead of by people like her mother, who believed that everyone should look out for everyone else.

For all the anxiety it caused her, the train ride was short—only three kilometers from station to station. It had taken less time to travel to her destination than it had taken to watch the warning vids and sign all of the documentation.

Berhane received a small chip that certified she had agreed to all of the conditions, and that chip, she was told, was good for the next twelve months.

Apparently, chips like that made it possible for people to travel inside and outside of the dome with much more ease than she'd had this afternoon.

Once the train docked at the warehouse station, the doors opened and everyone on board disembarked. There were only four passengers at this time of day. The trains only ran hourly between ten am and two pm; after that, they would run on fifteen minute cycles until some kind of shift change occurred that Berhane wasn't privy to.

She remained on the platform long after the train left. She faced a white wall with Armstrong Search & Rescue's red-and-blue logo emblazoned across it. The doors leading into the facility were also blue and red.

She hadn't let anyone know she was coming; she wondered if that was a mistake. She suddenly worried that no one was even here.

For once, she doubted the information she had looked up at home. Maybe she would have to wait in this nothingness until the next train arrived.

The only way to find out, of course, was to go into the facility.

So she walked to the double doors as if she had done it a million times before. She pushed on them with both hands. They swung open, and she found herself inside a warm room with some blaring music. She didn't recognize it, although it was melodic and comprised mostly of brass Earth instruments.

Tables strewn with equipment she didn't recognize stood against walls. There were no chairs, and no obvious place for visitors to go.

"Hello?" she called.

One minute. The message that crossed her links was written in Standard and did not appear to be automated. Someone had contacted her through her public net, probably through some kind of program.

Come around to the back, said the next message.

Wherever the back was. Just as she had that thought, a map appeared in a box to the side of her right eye.

She followed the red highlighted route. It took her past pallets of equipment, most of which she didn't recognize, and past piles of emergency medical kits, the kind that Aristotle Academy used to take on field trips.

The pallets formed a maze. She couldn't see beyond all of the stuff. It made her feel oddly claustrophobic and a little lonely. She had come here to be with like-minded people, not to wander through a full warehouse in search of someone to talk to.

She finally rounded a corner into a corridor. The red highlighted route seemed redundant here. There was only one way for her to go.

She went through an open door, and there she saw a tall man with graying hair that brushed against his collar. He was too thin, not in the enhanced, egotistical way of social climbers and the wealthy, but in a way she rarely saw among her friends—he looked like he often forgot to eat.

He extended a hand. "Dabir Kaspian."

She shook it. His fingers were warm, dry, and a little boney. "Berhane Magalhães."

"It's not often we get a donor here." Something in his tone told her that he thought she was inspecting where her money had gone. Which explained the route she had taken. She thought it had felt circuitous. It had been, so she could see the pallets of supplies.

"I'm not here as a donor," she said. "I want to volunteer."

The look he gave her was momentarily cold. She recognized it, and its message: *I don't have time to train a do-gooder.*

"What kind of skills do you have?" he asked, his tone filled with practiced warmth.

"I have no medical training, but I'm physically strong. I can lift things, move things, and shout when I find something." She tried not to sound sarcastic.

"We have bots for that," he said.

"No, you don't," she said. "I read about the recovery effort that you're doing. There's a worry that the bots won't respect the dead, no matter how well programmed they are."

He let out a small, half-amused sound. "Well," he said, "that's more than most people come in here knowing."

He stepped away from the door and let her walk all the way into the room. It was a small office. Every wall had an array of screens, and all of them showed a different section of rubble. The images were so close-in that Berhane couldn't tell exactly where they were, only that they were live.

In the midst of all of them were workers in the red-and-yellow Search & Rescue environmental suits provided gratis by the Earth Alliance. Nearby, bots lifted and moved debris, placing it on floating platforms that would take it outside the dome. Out there, someone or something would determine what could be recycled and what needed to be buried or jettisoned.

She had seen a small pile of debris like that form outside of Armstrong after the bombing four years ago. In some ways, that little pile had been more offensive than the ruins inside the dome. She often found herself worrying whether bits of her mother were still in it, since her mother's body had never been recovered.

She took a deep shaky breath.

"Who did you lose?" Kaspian's voice was soft, sympathetic, and unlike that practiced warmth of a moment ago, sounded quite genuine.

She said without thinking, "My mother."

Then her cheeks heated. Her mother had been dead a long time now. Berhane turned, then moved her hands slightly, as if she could take back her words.

"I'm sorry," she said. "You meant last week. Who did I lose last week?"

"Yes," he said, a frown on his weathered face. For the first time, she noticed that he was oddly good-looking. His hollowed cheekbones and heavy bone structure made him resemble those old-Earth Romantic Poets she'd been studying just last week, poets whose words had seemed so profound and now seemed…irrelevant. Or perhaps something less important than they had been.

Something that would wait for her to have a life of leisure again.

"I didn't lose anyone close last week," she said, her voice trembling, not just with embarrassment, but also with the sadness she had felt as she looked at the debris. "My mother died in the first bombing, four years ago."

"Oh." In that single word, Kaspian conveyed a lot of understanding and a bit of compassion. Or maybe that was all conveyed by his extremely expressive face. "So you understand."

She nodded. "My father just wants to move forward, rebuild, pretend like these crises can be paved over."

"There's an argument to be made for going ahead," Kaspian said. "Some believe it's the only option."

Berhane glanced over her shoulder at the images on that wall.

"Millions of people are missing," she said quietly. "We all assume they're dead, but I can tell you, as someone who has been through this, there's a tiny part of your brain that thinks, 'Oh, they're just missing' or 'they ran away' or 'they Disappeared.' It's a little bit of hope that, over time, becomes almost destructive."

The heat in her cheeks grew. She wasn't used to revealing herself to strangers like this.

"When we got Mother's DNA, and when they told us where it was found, I grieved all over again. Maybe more fully." Her voice shook. "But I finally got rid of the hope. I *knew* she was gone. And I think, strangely enough, that was an actual blessing."

Kaspian studied her for a moment, then nodded. He was good at this. He didn't patronize her with any false platitudes, nor did he force some religious nonsense on her.

Instead, he glanced at the wall, that sympathetic expression still on his face.

"I'm one of the managers of this office," he said, still watching the volunteers out there, working. "In different times, you would have received some kind of thank-you message from us, and we would have brought you here for a tour as a major donor."

"I'm not—"

"Please, Ms. Magalhães, let me finish."

She bit her lower lip. She was used to taking over conversations, not listening to them. She nodded once.

"I understand how this has revived your grief. I respect that. I also understand your need to do something." He moved away from the screens, his gray eyes now meeting hers. There was a lot of very real sympathy in his gaze. "But there are a million ways to help, and you've been helping in the one way that most people can't. You've already given hundreds of thousands to the rescue effort, and I can't imagine that we were the only beneficiaries."

"Money is nothing," she said. "It's not—"

"Money is everything to an organization like this one. It buys the pallets and the equipment, gets the volunteers to the site, pays for medical care if some volunteer gets injured, pays for DNA testing the domes won't do, really, Ms. Magalhães, money is more important than you can ever realize."

She nodded. She supposed she knew that. But it felt wrong. It felt dehumanizing. Especially with her father sitting in his dining room, planning to replenish the coffers that she was emptying, and doing so in such a way as to obliterate some of the work that Armstrong S&R needed to do.

"I don't plan to stop giving financially," she said. "But it's not enough. For me, anyway. I need to do some hands-on work. I've never been in a situation where the whole Moon is in crisis, and I can't do much—"

"Ms. Magalhães…"

"It's my turn," she said softly. "I've been very lucky in my life. I was raised in wealth and privilege. I don't need to work. I have more than enough money to last me and mine forever, and I didn't earn it. Let me do this."

He studied her for a long minute. "Do you know what you're asking?"

"Not completely," she said. "I suspect I won't know until I'm out there, working my ass off."

He chuckled. The sound seemed rusty, as if he hadn't done that for a long time. Maybe he hadn't.

"All right," he said. "But I have to warn you, we have liability waivers that'll take you all day to read and sign."

She smiled. "You mean in addition to the ones I had to sign just to get here."

He didn't smile back.

"Yes," he said. "It's risky in these damaged domes. The debris isn't stable, and anything can puncture an environmental suit. Our suits close up pretty fast, but no one knows what'll get inside even in that short space of time. We have no idea if we're dealing with chemicals we haven't seen or bacteria or—"

"It's all right," she said. "I want the risk."

He sighed. "Just as long as wanting the risk doesn't make you reckless."

"I'm sure you'll keep me in line if that is the case," she said.

"In line?" he said. "No, I won't do that. I'll pull you out of the field and won't let you back. I don't care how much you donate."

She believed him. And she actually welcomed it.

"Give me those forms," she said. "The sooner I fill them out, the sooner I can get to work."

16

FINALLY, *FINALLY*, THE PORT OF ARMSTRONG LET SELECTED SHIPS LAND. Wilma Goudkins cheated: she used her Earth Alliance Security Division credentials to expedite the landing, even though she wasn't here on government business.

This was as personal as it could get.

After Anniversary Day—after she had seen what had happened to Tycho Crater (*heard* what had happened, dammit, Carla)—she had booked the first flight for this solar system out of the starbase housing the Security Division. She hadn't been alone; the flight was filled with Earth Alliance employees who had taken emergency leave to see what had become of their families.

Each person on this flight was grateful that she had used her credentials to jump the line in orbit around the Moon. Each person probably figured she was the one who would be fired for using government resources on a personal mission.

And she really didn't care.

Just like she hadn't cared that her boss disapproved of her leave.

Her sister had just died, most likely (although Goudkins hoped—hoped against hope—that the lapse in communication late that day had been caused by some technical problem), and Goudkins' supervisor wanted her to stay until there was confirmation.

Goudkins threatened to appeal. After she had snapped, *If I wait, then I miss the funeral,* even though she didn't know if there was going to be a funeral. If anyone was going to have a funeral.

As she got closer to the Moon, and the pilots announced that the Port of Armstrong *still* wasn't letting in ships, she began to realize just how big a mess she was walking into.

Alone.

Her family mostly lived on Earth, but they were distant cousins and an aunt and uncle she had met only once. Her sister Carla hadn't married, and had no children.

Goudkins had married and divorced before she and her husband had the two or three children they had hoped for.

She knew the difference between hope and reality; she had lived it every day of that marriage—hoping for one of those perfect relationships that some couples managed, and discovering that reality consisted of two people who simply couldn't get along, no matter how much they wanted to.

It was a small thing to compare to the evisceration of the Moon, but it was her small thing—and her greatest hurt after the death of her parents.

Her greatest hurt until now.

She and Carla had always been close. Her mother used to call them almost-twins—only 11 months apart. Goudkins was the younger and she couldn't remember a time in her life without Carla.

They'd been sharing a link that horrible day.

Carla had been in the Top of the Dome, a resort built against the dome in Tycho Crater, when the attacks started. Carla contacted Goudkins, asked for her advice on how to deal with the crisis, and had managed to escape the resort and the madman who had taken people hostage.

Then she had gone back in to help with the rescue, to help with the victims. She was leading first responders inside when Goudkins lost contact with her.

Later, Goudkins learned she had lost contact at the exact moment the bomb destroying the resort had gone off.

Still, she hoped—there was that word again, *hope*—that her sister had maybe been lying to her or that she had misunderstood where Carla really had been. Maybe her sister was injured in one of the local hospitals or so busy with reviving her city that she hadn't had time to get her links repaired, hadn't had time to contact her sister, figuring Goudkins would understand.

And maybe Goudkins would have if the circumstances were different, if the incident was isolated, or if she had been closer.

Maybe she would have done the same thing in Carla's place.

She didn't know.

What she did know was this: her sister and best friend was missing, presumed dead, and she would never forgive herself if she didn't investigate in person.

That's what Goudkins was trained in—investigation. And she had investigated a thousand crimes for the Alliance. She had met thousands of victims who wanted to believe the best, even when faced with the worst.

She knew she was behaving just like them, and she knew she couldn't stop.

As the ship was cleared to land in the Earth Alliance-only terminal of the Port of Armstrong, she took her seat. She started scanning available hotel rooms in Tycho Crater, hoping (again!) she would find something.

So far, she had been shut out. Most of the hotels in Tycho Crater had been near the Top of the Dome resort, and that meant most of them had been destroyed.

She had hoped she would find something, but she was coming up short.

Which meant that she'd have to pull rank again. Not to displace someone from a hotel room, but to get one of the apartments reserved for visiting dignitaries.

She didn't want to contact Dominic Hanrahan, the mayor of Tycho Crater. He'd been one of the targets of assassination and had somehow survived. He would have his hands full.

Plus, he would assume that she was in Tycho Crater on Earth Alliance business, not personal business.

She wasn't sure how to walk that fine line between using her credentials to get her way and obligating her employers to something they hadn't yet agreed to do.

She didn't look at the other passengers in the waiting area on the ship. She couldn't quite face them. They'd all spent more time than they'd planned together, in the time they'd been circling the damn Moon. They'd had conversations they would probably regret someday, sharing memories, sharing fears, sharing gossip and news and rumor.

Once this ship secured its berth in the port, they'd all scatter across the Moon and would probably never see each other again.

She knew better than to wish them luck. She would have gotten angry if they had wished her luck.

So she gripped the arm rests, leaned her head back, and prayed she'd see her sister again.

17

HUỲNH TOOK OFF THE STUPID ENVIRONMENTAL SUIT AND USED SOME extra nanocleaners to scrub her face. She wished she had the ability to clean the insides of her mouth and nose. She felt contaminated by the suit, or maybe by the encounter with Xyven.

The restroom near the environmental suits was cold, but then her body temperature always felt a bit off when she removed an environmental suit. It was as if her body's regulatory system took a vacation every time she put a suit on, letting the suit regulate the comfort level rather than her body communicating what kind of comfort it needed.

She looked in the bank of mirrors that covered the only unblocked wall. If she wanted to wash her hands or splash water on her face, she had to wave her hand over a little sign in the middle of the mirror that said *Sink* in whatever language the user needed.

She needed a sink. Her hair—so nicely coiffed and purple-tinged when she left her apartment—did look like someone had spilled dye all over it and then frizzed each strand.

She waved over the sign, then with a wave of her hand over the faucet, she turned on the hot water. It smelled faintly of roses, which irritated her. That would probably clash with her perfume. So she had two choices: she could comb her hair and hope for the best; or she could use water to tame her hair.

She opted for a third choice. Comb first, water second. It kinda worked. Her face was still flushed, and her purple fingernails had turned darker than she remembered. Or maybe she had picked the wrong color after all.

She adjusted her earrings and her dress. She still looked like she had just gotten out of bed after a night of hard drinking.

She sorta felt that way too.

Damn Xyven. His lack of vision would cost him one day.

The problem was that she might not be around to revel in it.

She ran a hand over her unruly hair one last time, then commanded the sink to retract. She slung the environmental suit over her arm and let herself out of the bathroom.

"Hey, Ava!"

She started at the voice, and turned slightly. Lawrence Ostaka stood near the door. He looked even more rumpled than usual, his shirt bagging around the fat he wore around his waist like a belt.

She let out a private sigh as she put on her professional I'm-in-charge face. "Lawrence," she said. "You need to call me Ms. Huỳnh now, remember?"

"Sorry," he said, but she knew he didn't mean it.

She had been promoted over him two years ago, and he always treated her like she was still the new hire. She was, compared to him. He had at least ten years more on the job than she did, but he had stalled due to his poor people skills.

He was a fantastic investigator, though, with a closure rate that rivaled Xyven's. Having Ostaka on her team kept her closures high. She valued that.

She also sent him on a lot of jobs, ostensibly because of those high closure rates, but also because he unnerved her.

Sometimes she wondered if he was stalking her or if he just wanted her to feel uncomfortable and complain about him. She thought it might be the latter, which was why she didn't report him. She didn't want to get into a he-said she-said situation with Lawrence Ostaka. She had a hunch his meticulous investigation skills would carry over into any conflict he had with another employee—particularly a superior—and quite frankly, she hadn't cared enough about him to meticulously record every single thing he had done to irritate her.

"Xyven didn't want to do a joint investigation, huh?" Ostaka said.

She started and for a moment, wondered how Ostaka had known that. Then she smiled herself. She could be so clueless sometimes. Duh. Of course, he had known that she wanted a joint investigation. Why else would she come to this part of the base?

"What brings you here, Lawrence?" she asked, taking advantage of the fact that she didn't have to use his last name.

She knew she was being a bit passive-aggressive. Her behavior was less about Ostaka than it was about Xyven, and she knew that too. She didn't care at the moment.

"Honestly," he said in a tone that put her on guard. People who said *honestly* like that often meant just the opposite, "I was here to volunteer for whatever assignment you were going for."

She frowned at him. "You followed me?"

"Yeah," he said.

She was surprised he had admitted it so easily, and was about to say so, but he hadn't finished.

"I was coming to your office to see if you had something new for me. I've been back on the base for nearly a month. Usually you send me somewhere new before now."

This time, she let her surprise show. He was right: she usually did try to reassign him quickly because she found him so very annoying.

She had gotten sidetracked with the entire Moon investigation thing.

She pushed past him just a little so that she could hang up the suit. As she did so, she made sure she placed it on the extra cleaning rack. She had hit the suit's automatic cleaning cycle, but she hated leaving any DNA behind, so she always set the suits she wore on the automated cleaning rack.

"And," he added when she still hadn't spoken, "I've never done a Joint Unit investigation. I'd love to see how some of the other investigators work."

"I wish I could help you there," she said. "Xyven and I don't have a joint investigation going."

"Then why were you visiting him?"

She turned.

"Lawrence, you want to rethink that question?"

His face fell just a bit. She didn't like it when he did the "I'm so innocent" thing. It never worked. He didn't have the ability or the personality to pull it off.

"I'm just—is there something you can assign me to? Because this Moon bombing thing has me antsy. I'd love to go to the Moon to investigate."

"Wouldn't we all?" she asked. "I'll see what's up next on the rotation, and let you know, all right?"

"You're not tasked with running that investigation?" he asked in such a way that let her know he already knew she was in charge of that investigation.

"Excuse me," she said, and pushed past him. Then she headed down the corridor at her normal clip.

She turned up her hearing enhancement, listening for his footsteps in case he was following her. As far as she could tell without looking, he wasn't.

She knew she shouldn't be so annoyed by him, but she was.

And because she was, she wasn't going to assign him to the Moon. She would set up her own teams without Lawrence Ostaka.

She had an investigation in Valhalla Dome that needed a second eye. She'd send him there. He'd close that case faster than the original investigator.

She probably wasn't making the most professional decisions regarding Ostaka, but she didn't care.

He'd annoyed her one too many times, and she didn't need the distraction right now.

She checked her links as she walked, trying to see just how fast she could get him off this base.

Because the sooner he was gone, the better she would feel.

18

DABIR KASPIAN WOULDN'T LET HER WORK RIGHT AWAY. BERHANE UNDERSTOOD, really she did, but she felt an underlying frustration. She *wanted* to work. She *needed* to work.

He wanted her to change her mind.

He didn't say that in so many words—or maybe he did. After scanning the forms she had filled out, he had said, *You won't be assigned field work until you've finished training, and training won't start for two more days. If things change in those few days, please feel free to let us know.*

She had almost told him in no uncertain terms that of course she would return, and no, she wouldn't change her mind, but something stopped her. Maybe it was the realization that his words were less about her than they were about the experiences he'd had with Armstrong S&R. Or maybe she finally understood this was about not pissing off a donor, and dealing with volunteers.

She had smiled at him, asked him what time he needed her, and then thanked him. She didn't ask him for the shorter way out of the warehouse.

She wanted to see all those supplies again, to know exactly where her donations were going.

The red lines of the map had reappeared in front of her eyes. She could tell immediately that the track back was shorter. Kaspian had updated her exit routes without her even asking.

She blinked the new route away and asked her system to let her retrace her steps.

The lines vanished, then reappeared, adding a good ten minutes onto her walk.

She added more, threading her way through the pallets of material. She was nearly to the door when she heard someone curse.

She started. "Sorry?" she said, then wondered if she should even have spoken up. Maybe she shouldn't have brought attention to herself.

A man peered around a pallet covered with dried food packages. He held a small, ancient scanner in his right hand. His straight black hair flopped over his forehead.

She had seen him before; she knew she had. It took her a moment to place him.

The port. Fiona's father. What was his name? Donal. Donal Ó Brádaigh, he had said, with just a bit of a lilt in his voice.

"Mr. Ó Brádaigh?" Berhane asked.

He stepped into the small aisle between pallets. The effect was startling. The narrowness of the aisle made his shoulders seem broader than she remembered, but the height of the pallets made him seem short. She had remembered him being taller than she was.

"Ms. Magalhães?" he said. "What are you doing here?"

"I could ask the same of you." She walked toward him, even though she probably should have been leaving.

He was taller, just like she remembered.

"I'm just finishing up," he said.

"You work here?" she asked.

He wasn't wearing any kind of identifying clothing. What he was wearing had some black stains along the ankles and thighs, and some heavy wear on the knees. He also wore work boots that looked like they were older than he was.

"Volunteer," he said. "When I can."

"When your wife can watch your daughter," Berhane said, understanding in her voice.

His cheeks turned a dusty shade of red. "No," he said. "I'm afraid my wife is gone."

Gone. Berhane didn't know what that meant exactly, but he said the word with such sadness she wasn't sure she should ask.

"I'm sorry," she said.

"No need to be sorry. It's been four years." Even though something in his voice made it sound like yesterday.

Berhane frowned just a little. Wasn't little Fiona about four? But Berhane had been nosy enough.

"I didn't mean to bother you," she said. "I was just on my way out."

"It's all right," he said. "I'm just waiting for the next train. I thought I'd get a bit more scanning done before it showed up."

Berhane looked over her shoulder. "How do you know when it gets here?"

"There are announcements," he said. "This place is so huge, we don't want anyone to miss a train and get stuck here."

Echoing her thoughts from her arrival. She nodded, hoping she didn't look quite as nervous as she felt.

"First time here?" he asked.

"Yeah," she said.

"Inspecting where your money is going?" Somehow he didn't make the question sound rude. It seemed routine.

"No," she said. "I want to go to work."

"It's rather dull, scanning things in the warehouse," he said.

"I…was hoping to be in the field."

His eyebrows went up. He snapped a finger and a serving bot showed up, floating down the aisle, its top a flat tray. He set the scanner on the tray, and the bot disappeared.

"Why don't they scan?" she asked, nodding toward the bot.

"We need eyeballs on everything," he said. "Since we're working with volunteers, we have to make sure they don't 'accidentally' compensate themselves with some of our supplies, and then fudge the system to cover it."

"Can't someone set up an inventory system that's hard to fudge?" she asked.

"Sure," he said. "For a lot of money. And then that someone would have to update it. It wouldn't be volunteer friendly."

"But wouldn't the volunteers be better off in the field—"

"Not everyone can handle the field," he said. "And a lot of people are like you. They want to do something, but they might only have an hour here or an hour there. They can scan things or help with the ordering or make sure the right supplies are on the right train. There's so much more to do here than we could ever manage. Especially now."

She nodded. She wondered if some of the people who couldn't "handle" the field had tried, or if Kaspian and his crew washed them out in training.

She would find out, she supposed.

"Do you work here?" she asked.

He smiled. "No. I volunteer."

"It's clear you didn't just join up after Anniversary Day," she said.

His smile faded. "I've been here a while. Less than I want, but more than I should, probably, given Fee."

It took Berhane a moment to realize he meant his daughter, Fiona, and not some fee for working here.

"Your daughter is special," she said.

"I like to think so," he said.

An announcement for the next train into Armstrong sounded overhead and across her links. It would leave ten minutes from now.

"I guess we should go," he said.

She nodded and let him lead her out of the warehouse of pallets. She kept the map on in her links though; she was beginning to wonder if she would ever entirely trust anyone.

He was leading her the way the map showed.

They reached the platform. The train waited, silver coated with gray Moon dust. No one sat inside the car.

Ó Brádaigh gestured with his hand, as if he were holding a door open for her. She smiled at him and boarded first.

He followed, and hesitated as if he wasn't sure if he should sit near her. After a moment, he sat across from her.

"I'm kind of amazed you want to go in the field," he said.

She shrugged a shoulder. "I want to contribute."

"There are other ways to contribute." He sounded like Kaspian.

"Yes," she said, "and I'm doing them. But they don't feel like enough."

Ó Brádaigh studied her for a moment. "Guilt?" he asked softly.

She stiffened. "What do you mean?"

"It just seems like a reaction... I don't know. I'm sorry. That was presumptuous of me."

The train beeped. A warning flashed across her links that the train would leave in less than a minute.

No one else joined them on the train.

"What was?" she asked.

"That, you know, I thought, maybe you..." He shook his head again.

"I'm feeling guilty because I'm rich and privileged?" she asked, careful not to sound bitter.

"No, I was thinking, sometimes when a major crisis happens, we feel like if we could just do something, then we can make up for surviving it." He looked down. "Or, at least, I do."

She was going to argue with him until that last sentence, uttered so softly she almost missed it.

Did she want to explain herself to this man? She didn't even know him, yet she felt like she did.

"I...um...yeah, that's probably a component," she said. "My mother died four years ago. In the first bombing."

He raised his head. His expression was...quizzical? Fascinated? She couldn't quite tell.

"Look," he said, "I don't have to pick up Fee for another hour. Can I buy you a cup of coffee?"

A cup of coffee. No one had offered to buy her coffee while on a train since her mother's last morning.

Berhane felt a pang deep in her heart. She almost said no. And because she almost said no, she made herself smile.

"I'd like that," she said.

19

"FIRST," THE GIRL SAID, "YOU TELL ME WHAT A FAMOUS RICH GUY LIKE YOU is doing here."

Deshin stared at her, activating one of his chips. She was clearly Pietres' daughter. Then she figured out who Deshin was. Most people in Armstrong had heard of him, but not seen him. It was rare for him to be recognized outside of the city or the Moon's business community.

But that didn't mean much. If she paid attention to people like her father or people who had done business with her father in the past, she might know who Deshin was.

So he launched a quick search of his internal databases, to make sure she was who she said she was.

He also checked for a record of Pietres's death. That came up immediately and confirmed what she told Deshin: Pietres had died a week before Anniversary Day, but no cause was listed.

The lights had finally turned completely on in the small storefront. It was cluttered and dusty, filled with unlabeled vials and boxes. Some rocks and gems glittered on one shelf, a few bound books were stacked on another. He'd worked with books like that before. Their pages were often coated with poisons that were best transferred on paper.

In this place, he knew better than to touch anything with his bare hands. He had warned Jakande about the same thing, and he hoped Jakande remembered.

Jakande was focused on Deshin and the girl, standing a half step behind Deshin, and probably turned slightly so that he could see the door as well as the girl behind the counter.

Deshin didn't turn to look, so he didn't know for certain. He just knew how Jakande did his job.

The search on the girl came back slowly—the private network that Deshin used was having trouble getting power down here. But it was a tribute to the network that it could work even in this place. Deshin would wager that most people's private networks didn't work at all in Pietres's storefront.

According to the search, the girl's name was Ethelina. She was twenty-two, and she was the only surviving member of Pietres's family. His sons had been killed more than a decade ago, and his wife had died twenty years before.

Deshin had known none of that before now, even though he had done business with Pietres more recently than twenty-five years ago. Of course, Deshin hadn't done the business face to face. He had made the contact, then had his people handle things.

Pietres had been in a dangerous business, and the collateral damage that had been his family simply showed it.

"Ethelina," Deshin said, and the girl started. Her colorless eyes grew wide. She hadn't expected him to find her name at all. "Tell me what happened to your father."

She bit her upper lip. To her credit, she didn't look in any direction or even seem to access her links. That, more than anything, told Deshin that she was alone down here, and that no one else had hacked the business or the business's networks.

She swallowed hard, then glanced at Jakande.

"You may as well trust me," Deshin said. "Because no one else is going to help you out. Since your family is gone and your father didn't make many friends, you're going to have to try to run his business on your own. And believe me, a protected kid who went to the Moon's best schools wasn't trained to run this kind of work, not with the kind of people you'll run into."

She swallowed hard again. "People like you, Mr. Deshin?"

He smiled. It was an old smile, one he rarely used any more. Half charm, half menace. It used to have quite an impact on women all those years ago. They saw the charm and discounted the menace. Men often saw only the menace and discounted the charm.

She glanced at Jakande again, then back at Deshin. She had apparently noticed both the charm and the menace, because the attitude she had shown just a moment before faded.

He waited. She would come around. She had no one, and she was scared. She'd already made two mistakes in this conversation, and if she thought it through, she would realize what those mistakes were.

"If I tell you what happened to my father, will you leave me alone?" she asked.

"If you want me to," Deshin said, and meant it. *He* would leave her alone. But he might send a business associate here to try to buy out the last of Pietres' stock and his stored information.

Deshin wasn't going to tell her that, though.

She swallowed a third time. It seemed to be an involuntary response, a tell, something that would destroy her in this business.

He couldn't help himself: He thought of Paavo, and how unsuited the boy would be at her age if Deshin had died without training him. (Even if Deshin did train him; Paavo was marching on a similar education track to the one Ethelina had marched.)

"I killed him," she said, and that caught Deshin's attention like nothing else had. His hand moved ever so slightly closer to the pistol he carried under his suit coat.

Jakande had stiffened beside him, clearly ready to pull Deshin out of the building if need be.

"How did you kill him?" Deshin asked softly.

Her face crumpled. "I thought he was so handsome."

It took Deshin a moment to realize she had meant a different "he."

"Now they're everywhere," she said.

Jakande let out an involuntary "huh?" but Deshin understood.

"You brought one of the Anniversary Day clones down here?" Deshin asked.

Jakande turned quickly enough that Deshin saw it. Surprise.

I'll take care of the conversation, he sent to Jakande. It was a reprimand.

Deshin hadn't reprimanded him for his lack of attention on Anniversary Day, believing it understandable. But Jakande had been a bit off ever since that massive bombing, and Deshin needed him on his game.

"I met him topside," she said of the clone. "There's a bar—it's mostly for tourists, but I'd been here since I graduated, and I was getting so tired of Gerlache. There's nothing in this place except criminals and failures."

Deshin privately agreed. But he didn't say anything, letting her talk. His heart was pounding. He hadn't expected anyone to have talked with one of the clones, and she had.

"We hit it off. I was stupid," she said. "I didn't think he knew who I was, but he had to, right?"

It wasn't hard to find her, especially if someone was looking at Pietres's history. But Deshin didn't say that either. He inclined his head in encouragement.

"We—God, I thought he was a handsome man, brilliant, and I was lucky to meet someone like him here. I figured I'd meet someone in school, but I never did or they'd dump me for no reason—"

Oh, there probably had been a reason. If she had been Deshin's daughter, he would have had his people scare off anyone who hadn't been appropriate.

"—but he, he was so considerate." Those colorless eyes were lined with tears. She didn't brush them away, but she didn't blink either. "The next morning—I was so stupid. He was talking about love at first sight and romance and soul mates, and I believed him. I absolutely believed him."

She really wouldn't survive in this business if it had been that easy to get to her. Pietres should have been ashamed of himself, protecting her to that degree.

Then Deshin's skin warmed. He was probably letting Gerda do the same thing with Paavo.

But Paavo was seven, not twenty-two. Paavo had time to toughen up. This girl should have been tough by the time she came of age.

"He wanted to meet my dad, and I said we could meet at this restaurant topside, and we did, and Dad thought it was weird, but he kinda liked him, and then they talked and I don't know, they seemed to hit it off."

"Did he negotiate to buy anything from your dad at dinner?" Deshin asked.

"No," she said. "My dad would have told me to stay away from him then. My dad didn't want me to associate with his people or the people who did business with him. My dad would have chased him off if he wanted anything from this place."

"Then how do you know he killed your dad?" Deshin asked.

"Because the next day, before he left me, he said he had business and he'd be back, but he never came back. So I came here to talk to my dad, and I found him, and he was dead, and I called the police, but they didn't care—you know what Daddy did."

"I do," Deshin said softly.

She nodded. "They don't care about people like him and he knew it—"

The other "he" again, the boyfriend, the killer, the clone.

"—and that was how he could steal from my dad, and kill him, just like he killed Mayor Oliu."

Oliu. One of the mayors assassinated on Anniversary Day.

"The police didn't care that your father was killed with zoodeh?" Deshin asked. He was surprised. It was a banned substance, after all.

She gave him a contemptuous glance. "Where do you think you are, Armstrong? People die strangely here all the time. The police are paid to look the other way. I know. My father paid a bunch of them."

She shook her head, then let out a small laugh.

"I would have thought that those payments bought some loyalty, but I guess not. Not after death."

"Not even after Anniversary Day?" Deshin asked. "They didn't come back here? They didn't think it strange that your father died the way that the mayor died, only one week earlier?"

"They probably haven't even noticed." Her voice shook. "Or maybe they just don't care."

"You didn't contact them about it?"

She shook her head. "They've been mostly working in Sverdrup Crater. And they already made it clear that they weren't going to do anything about my dad. So what's the point of trying?"

One of the tears dripped off her unblinking eye. She wiped at the tear, then shook her head, and blinked. More tears fell, and she brushed at them furiously, as if they had betrayed her.

"You still haven't told me how you knew that one of the clones killed your father."

"Because we have security here," she snapped. "He bought zoodeh from Dad, then tested it on Dad. I watched it all. More than once. Those clones are brutal, Mr. Deshin. They're not just robots doing a job. He seduced me, and attacked Dad, and it took a lot of thought. I mean, Daddy didn't even throw him out of here when he asked for the zoodeh. He told Daddy that he wouldn't see me again, and he apologized and said he never meant for it to happen, and Daddy *believed* him. Daddy doesn't believe anybody."

She hiccupped, and shook her head.

"Didn't," she said. "Didn't believe anybody."

Deshin let out a small breath. He hadn't expected any of that. "Let me see the footage," he said.

She shook her head. "Don't you understand? You're doing what he did. You're convincing me to trust you, to let you into the back, to let you close. You'll just kill me too."

Deshin smiled, his real smile this time. "I don't kill people," he said.

"If that were true, you wouldn't know my father," she said, and there was truth in that.

"I'm a respected businessman now," Deshin said.

"Who came alone with one bodyguard." She was smart, for all of her naiveté. But she didn't have time to learn her father's business, no matter how smart she was. And she was grieving, which made most people even more careless.

"I came alone to talk with your father. I know how little he trusted people," Deshin said.

"You came to him why?" she asked.

She'd been honest with him. Deshin had no doubt about that. Under other circumstances, that would have made Deshin more likely to tell her why he was here. But with Pietres dead, it didn't matter what he told her.

"Old business," Deshin said. He was unable to confess that he was searching for information on zoodeh. "Nothing I can tell you without you digging into ancient files, and even then, it's probably not worthwhile."

"It seems worthwhile," she said. "You came alone."

Deshin sighed. "Look, what I wanted from your father doesn't matter anymore. If you can send me the footage, I'd like to see it. I don't have to get near you—and you don't have to get near me. All right?"

She nodded, then shook her head a third time. "Ah, hell," she said, and waved her hand.

The screen she had been looking at before became visible. On it was one of the clones as Deshin had not seen them. He was dressed in an expensive black jacket with matching pants, his hair combed back. He looked wealthy and comfortable and exotic, precisely the kind of man that women who liked danger would find attractive.

I came down here to apologize, the clone said to Pietres. *I met your daughter, and found her very appealing. I didn't realize she was your daughter until last night's dinner. Which makes this all so awkward. Because I prefer to keep my business life and my personal life separate. Unfor-*

tunately, my time is not my own this week.

A mixture of truth and lies, the way the very best con men worked. Deshin frowned. He'd never heard one of the clones speak. He was surprised at the slight hint of an accent—one he couldn't place—and the clipped, educated tone.

He glanced over the top of the screen at the girl. She was wiping her face with the back of her hand, the tears still flowing, much to her obvious exasperation.

You do business with me or you speak to my daughter, Pietres said, with a menace that would have made Deshin think twice about doing either. *You do not do both.*

I know, sir, and I'm very sorry. I'm afraid I'm going to have to complete the business, since I'm not here on my own behalf. I'll apologize to your daughter—

You won't speak to her again.

Deshin watched the corners, the edges of the security video. He saw nothing out of the ordinary. The store looked the same.

The men discussed business. The clone asked for a small amount of zoodeh and a delivery and storage system. Before they settled on a price, Pietres told the clone about all of the difficulties in using zoodeh—from its instability to the fact that many assassins who use it often accidentally kill themselves.

The girl didn't seem distressed by any of this. Either she had heard the security recording several times or she knew about zoodeh. Her tears had slowed. Now she occasionally rubbed her thumb underneath her eyelids, and tried to surreptitiously watch Deshin and Jakande.

Deshin returned his gaze to the screen. Pietres had a bot retrieve the zoodeh from the back of the store. The zoodeh was in a small, double-protected vial; the delivery system in a flat box with several tiny needles glinting in the light.

The clone leaned forward, hands floating above the supplies. He and Pietres haggled over money, and then the clone sent him money—which surprised the crap out of Deshin. He hadn't expected that.

He glanced at the girl, but she didn't seem to notice. He wondered if she had tried to trace that money or if it still existed.

He would worry about that later.

Instead, he watched the screen. The clone thanked Pietres profusely, then apologized, seemingly for the incident with the daughter, and extended a hand.

Deshin's stomach tightened.

Pietres shook the clone's hand and smiled. Then Pietres started to frown, looking confused. A grayness seeped through his entire body, and he toppled backwards, like a statue that had been pushed.

Sorry, the clone said again, but he didn't seem to be speaking to Pietres. Instead, the clone seemed to be speaking to the room—or maybe the security cameras.

Deshin frowned. This was strange, no matter how he thought about it.

On screen, the clone slipped off gloves that had covered his hands, then put on a different pair of gloves—obvious gloves this time, where the original gloves had matched his skin perfectly.

He picked up the zoodeh and the delivery system, put them in a bag he had brought with him, and then pocketed them.

After one last look around the room, he left.

"Do you still have the money?" Deshin asked.

The girl looked at him, the blood leaving her skin. "Are you accusing me of something?"

"No," he said, but assigned that thought to consider later. "I want to know if you ever checked to see if the money made it into your accounts."

"I—yes, it's there. I don't know what to do with it." Her voice trembled.

Deshin nodded. He glanced at that screen. The whole interaction seemed strange. Or maybe that was hindsight.

After all, criminal interactions were often odd.

"He never gave his name," Deshin said, "at least not on your security vid here."

"He called himself Syv," she said. "I thought it was short for Sylvester or something."

"But you don't think that now?" Deshin asked.

She shook her head. "I looked that up at least. In one of the Earth dialects, it means seven."

Deshin shuddered despite himself. "Which Earth dialect?"

"Norwegian," she said. "It's spoken in places where the natives are pale and blond, like the clones."

Was that a coincidence? Deshin didn't know.

But he would try to find out.

20

"I FOUND HER IN THE GARDEN."

The voice belonged to Rahim Visso, the advanced math teacher. He sounded both worried and winded.

Pippa Landau felt dizzy. Her knees ached, and so did her head. She was supine, eyes closed, mouth dry, her back resting against something comfortable, pillows beneath her neck.

"Pippa?" A hand touched her face. The hand was soft and smelled of lavender. Pippa didn't recognize the voice or the hand or the lavender scent. "I think she fainted."

"I know she passed out," Rahim said, not hiding his sarcasm. "I did a medical scan. Her vitals seem fine, but I'm wondering if we should call for help of some kind."

"I'm all right." Pippa managed to speak, even though her lips didn't part well. She forced herself to open her eyes. The room—the teacher's lounge—spun. She closed her eyes again. She wasn't really all right.

She sent a message through her system. *Repair equilibrium.* Sometimes she felt like she should add a *please,* just in case some perverse part of her was holding back.

The dizziness ceased. She couldn't tell the staff here that her medical implants were less sophisticated than theirs. They'd want to know why, and she couldn't tell them the truth about her childhood.

She hadn't told anyone.

She opened her eyes again, saw the recessed lighting, the sketch of the Mississippi flowing along the ceiling. The room smelled of coffee and cinnamon, and the oval clock on the wall—a historic curiosity that everyone wanted to keep—said she still had half an hour before the students arrived.

"Are you all right, Pippa?" Rahim leaned over her, his narrow face constricted with worry. He had the nicest brown eyes. She had always thought that, but he was young, as young as her eldest child. Not, Rahim had said one day, that age should matter when humans lived so long.

"I think so," she said, and struggled to sit up.

"What happened?" he asked.

What lie could she tell? She wasn't thinking clearly enough to come up with one. Her brain was full of cloned men, made from a serial killer, marching out of her nightmares and onto the Moon.

She settled for, "I don't know." Then she gave Rahim a weak smile. "I'll be all right."

"If you need someone to take your classes..." the woman spoke.

Pippa looked at her, saw a heavyset woman with black hair threaded with gray, knew from the handmade clothes that the woman was one of those anti-technology types who had settled near the Amish communities west of here.

"I'll be fine," Pippa said. It was the first day of summer session. Her favorite. She had to remember that. "Just give me a few minutes."

Rahim shot her a worried look, but stepped back. He took the woman's arm and moved her out of the way as well.

Pippa sat up slowly. The question wasn't whether or not she would be all right. The question was should she talk to someone in authority? She had been running from those clones for her entire life, it seemed, even though she hadn't seen one since she was twenty-five. An entire lifetime ago.

She ran a hand over her face.

What could she tell anyone? That she had seen the clones more than thirty years ago? But the ones she had seen were dead now, and she had known nothing about them. They weren't even in the Alliance at the time, and they certainly weren't a threat to anyone.

Although the woman at the Disappearance Service had recommended a full Disappear, because she said someone could come after Pippa, and she would be easy to find under her real name. Since Pippa hadn't known what the clones wanted in the first place, she had had no idea if they would find her.

If they wanted to find her.

If they wanted to hurt her.

But clearly, this group hadn't thought of her. They had been on a mission, just like the clones she had seen so long ago.

She wanted to ask if they were fast-grow clones. But they had been laughing and interacting and traveling like cousins heading to a party. Fast-grow usually didn't engage each other like that. They would have been concentrated on the mission—if there was a mission, which these clones clearly had had.

She took a deep breath.

No one knew who she was. Not a soul on Earth, literally. Not her children. Not even her husband had known.

She had hidden effectively.

If she talked now, she could be found.

And as the woman at the Disappearance Service had said so long ago, *Do you want to test how badly they want to find you? Because we can give you a small package. If they find you, though, it'll be because you're searchable. We can make you impossible to find.*

Except for a Retrieval Artist, she had said, voice shaking.

They never succeed, the woman at the Disappearance Service had said. *They run scams. You have to worry about Trackers because they have access to government information, but Trackers can't find anyone we give a full Disappearance to either. I think your situation warrants it, but it's your choice. Remember. It's always your choice. And if you break your silence, you'll be easier to find.*

"Pippa?" Rahim asked, that frown on his face deepening. "Are you sure you shouldn't go home?"

It took her a moment to parse his sentence.

"I'm going to teach," she said. That was what she did now. What she had done for decades. She was Pippa Landau. She had a life here. A long life here.

Her family was here, she had lost no one, and nothing, in these recent attacks.

She had nothing to share except old, probably worthless information.

And that wasn't worth risking her entire existence for.

"Help me up," she said to Rahim, extending her hand. "I want to go back to the garden."

Where she was in charge. Where she could think about plants and ancient roses.

Where she would be safe.

21

EVEN THE TRAINS OUT OF THE PORT OF ARMSTRONG WERE CROWDED.

Goudkins stood, pressed against one of the walls in the joint human/alien part of the train. The bullet trains were segregated by species in the first class cars: that way each could enjoy the proper environment and accommodations.

Try as she might to get first class accommodations, she couldn't. She could barely get a ticket on the train. One of the port employees recommended that she go into Armstrong and get a different bullet train from another part of the city, and she might have considered it if she hadn't been able to get a ticket on this train.

The trains from the port were packed now that the ships were beginning to land. And everyone on these trains was trying to locate a loved one.

She recognized a few people from her ship, but she didn't do more than acknowledge them. They were scattered throughout the car, mixed between Rev and Peyti and a group of Flittabats that clung to the ceiling as if the car had been designed for them.

She kept her personal bag around her torso and her business bag inside the jacket she had brought along—not because she expected to be in a real "outside" environment like she would have been on Earth, but because she'd found that jackets were useful for storing things during travel, and even on starbases and in domed cities, no one looked at a jacket twice.

The stench inside the car was worse than she expected. Some of that was the Flittabats—they smelled rather strongly of rotted fruit—but some of it was nerves and close quarters. Humans had their own stink when they were stressed.

She hadn't been in quarters this close since she was promoted and sent off Earth. The Earth Alliance Security starbase had a low ratio of personnel to services, so not even at the busiest times was the public transportation crowded.

It would take hours to get from Armstrong to Tycho Crater, and she would have to stand the entire time. She could barely see out the windows, and what she did see—at least at first—seemed alarmingly normal.

Houses and businesses and restaurants, a dome that glowed with daylight colors, and a moonscape beyond.

She had known that Armstrong hadn't been hit this time, but she hadn't registered what that meant. It meant that life inside Armstrong seemed amazingly normal, while on the rest of the Moon, everyone panicked.

Or at least, she was imaging that they had panicked.

She was panicked, which angered her. She had too much training to be panicked. She knew how to keep her emotions in check.

And she was keeping them in check. But she could feel them seething underneath, and she felt that if she tapped them at all, she would erupt in some completely unpredictable way.

Dammit, Carla, she sent to her sister's unresponsive links for maybe the thousandth time. *Why did you have to go back into that resort? Why didn't you leave?*

So many people had escaped the Top of the Dome and headed just outside the part of the dome that sectioned—not on purpose. No one had expected that dome to section, so it couldn't be on purpose. If her sister had escaped whatever the hell had been happening in that resort, then she shouldn't have felt obligated to go back.

And Goudkins shouldn't have told her to go back.

She replayed that conversation again in her mind:

You're sure you're all right? she had sent to her sister.

There was a delay between the sending and the response. Communications with the starbase were expedited, just like everything within the Earth Alliance government, but it still took time for linked messages to cross the distance.

I'm uninjured, just a little scared, her sister had sent back.

It's normal to be scared, Goudkins had sent.

A lot of people are still there, Wilma, her sister had sent. *I'm thinking of going back in. You would, right?*

They had promised each other they would never lie. Not at all. And in the spirit of that, Goudkins had answered.

I would, she had sent.

And now she wished she had said, *You're not me. You have other skills. Stay out of the Top of the Dome. Do what you can on the ground. Let others go back in.*

But she hadn't sent that. She had communicated as best she could with her sister as Carla went back inside the resort.

Her last message had been a bit eerie: *I'm not sure what I'll find here, so I'm going to go dark. I don't know if they can listen in or if I'll trigger something. Wilma, in case—*

And it ended there.

Their entire conversation—their *lifelong* conversation—had ended there. At the exact moment a bomb had gone off, destroying the Top of the Dome resort, making it fall to the ground below, and creating a huge hole in the dome covering Tycho Crater.

A dome that had sectioned only moments before.

Goudkins always replayed that moment, that possibility that her sister had just shut down her links, the possibility that she hadn't been anywhere near the Top of the Dome, that she'd been having this conversation with Goudkins just outside that section, and the links had been severed because they were so precarious.

Because Goudkins didn't want to consider that her sister was inside the Top of the Dome. Nor did she want to think about her sister standing below it when the entire structure fell.

147

And she really didn't want to think about her sister watching the dome section and realizing—at the last moment—that she was on the wrong side of it.

Goudkins steeled herself.

The train had moved outside of Armstrong now, traveling so fast that the gray landscape blurred through the windows. Two stops between Armstrong and Tycho Crater. Just two on this line.

Announcements said they were nearing the first.

She hoped enough people got off the train to ease some pressure in the car.

Hope versus reality.

She wished she could stop playing that footage in her mind, but it was the difference between her trained brain and her conflicted heart.

Her supervisor had asked her why she wanted to come here, when there was the great possibility that her sister was dead and there would be no funerals for any of the dead on the Moon.

"I need to know," Goudkins had said.

That was reality.

She needed to know.

And soon, she would find out.

22

BOTHAINA ANGALL STOOD JUST INSIDE THE DOOR OF THE DANGEROUS Criminals Division of the Special DNA Collection Unit. Her skin tingled, and she was covered in sweat.

She hated what she called "reentry" and wished she could bring a lunch to work. She tried not to take her breaks, but her boss reminded her that she had to. Eight times per day she had to go through scrubbing and decontamination just to do her job. It left her skin raw, despite the enhancements she had received to cope with this, and the procedures didn't count putting on and removing her environmental suit, which sometimes scraped her raw skin.

She should have hated this job, but she didn't. The science fascinated her. Usually.

Today, though, she had an uneasy feeling in her stomach.

She had stopped just inside the door of the Dangerous Criminals Division, staring at the pillar in the center of the room. The pillars, scattered throughout the work area, didn't seem to hold up anything; they were there for design reasons only.

And propaganda reasons, as she had learned on her first day, five years ago.

Mostly, she ignored the pillars, but today, she couldn't.

She was staring at the small, round chamber built into the pillar to the left of the door. Inside that chamber was a double helix, looking like a ride at one of the amusement parks she had gone to on Earth as a child. The double helix, which was a 3-D model, was not an artist's rendering.

Instead, it showed every single detail of an existing person's DNA.

The Cautionary Tale, one of her colleagues called it.

The double helix mapped the DNA of one PierLuigi Frémont. It had been in the chamber for decades, long before Angall had even been born. She found that ironic, given today's news.

Except that it wasn't today's news. *She* had discovered the news today, but the rest of the Alliance had probably seen it much earlier.

The security footage of twenty clones of PierLuigi Frémont as they arrived in the Port of Armstrong had gone viral around the Alliance the moment the footage was released.

Angall had no relatives on the Moon, but she had traveled through that port dozens of times, the last time on her way to interview for this job. She even knew what part of the port those clones had arrived in.

They looked so normal, like a group of young men on some great adventure.

That was the most tragic part, as far as she was concerned: how normal they looked.

How normal this little strand of DNA looked. Like so many other double helixes, the differences weren't visible to the naked eye. And this double helix had no labels on its surface. Just one outside that little case, which had actually been painted onto the pillar.

*Dangerous Human DNA: Mass Murderer and Megalomaniac
PierLuigi Frémont*

The DNA, she had been told, existed there to remind her—to remind every human on the staff—that trouble could exist on the microscopic level. If they let even a speck of that DNA out of these labs, then bad things would happen.

Like nineteen explosions on the Moon, twelve domes damaged, millions of lives lost in an instant.

She shuddered to think about it, and yet no one here had mentioned it at all. Weren't they at fault? This DNA got out. It had escaped the Dangerous Criminals Division, and worse, it had done damage out there. Serious, bad damage.

(Damage wasn't even the word for it, not really.)

"Bother you?" Claudio Stott had come up beside her. He stopped a little too close, which he always did. He had fewer social skills than most of the people who worked here, but he was probably the best researcher and cataloguer in the lab.

As she turned toward him, she took a tiny step to the side. She made it all seem like one movement so that she wouldn't offend him.

Stott was taller than she was and pear-shaped. She had no idea how old he was, but he had been here long enough that his complexion had turned that olive-gold so many old-timers had, from the chemical showers they used to take coming in and out of the Special Collections Unit.

Those showers had been discontinued at least fifteen years ago, but the damage had been done. A few of the old-timers had gotten enhancements to improve their looks, but most of the older employees just didn't care.

A lot of humans inside this part of the Forensic Wing of the Earth Alliance Security Division didn't seem to care about the social niceties. Angall sometimes considered that a blessing—until one of those humans got a little too chummy.

"Doesn't it bother you?" she asked, not keeping her voice down the way that the staff was supposed to in the middle of the shift.

"No," he said, clasping his hands behind his back and looking at the spiral disappearing into the pillar.

"You know that his clones blew up the Moon, right?" she asked. "We failed, Claudio."

"Technically," he said softly, "the Moon is still there. And damage could have been so much worse. Imagine if those attacks had gone as planned, if the domes hadn't sectioned. Then life on the Moon as we know it would have been destroyed."

"I think it has been," Angall said. "Nothing will ever be the same."

"Well, the infrastructure is still there," Stott said. "Most of the inhabitants are still there. The *domes* are still there, if damaged. So, I stand by my statement and its corollary which is, life on the Moon can become normal again."

"I hope you're right," she said, mimicking his position. She put her hands behind her back, and stared at the DNA spiraling upward. "I still think we failed."

"We didn't fail," Stott said. "This incident simply proves how valuable we are."

"How do you figure?" Maureen Kamel left her post to join them. She was a short, dark woman who wore black clothes and black makeup that made her seem even darker.

"We make sure none of this material gets out," Stott said. "Now, we can probably lobby for more funding, because these clones have given the Alliance a useful example of how valuable the protections we offer truly are."

"Except that we didn't protect the DNA," Angall said. "It had to have come from us."

"No, it didn't come from us." Terri Muñoz had joined them. She had run the Division longer than most of them had been alive, and that probably included Stott.

She was wizened and her olive skin had a translucent quality. Her hands would occasionally shake as she worked, and then she'd have to go in for enhancement upgrades. Someone said the damage to her cells from all the chemicals she'd subjected them to simply couldn't be repaired.

"How do you know?" Stott was still staring at the DNA. If he hadn't asked the question, Angall would have thought he wasn't interested in the conversation at all.

Muñoz said, "I checked. We got notification from the Security Division days ago, when the footage first appeared, asking if we had a leak in the division."

Everyone tensed. They knew what a leak in the division meant. More work than they could do, inspectors everywhere, and the possibility for all kinds of work getting compromised.

The division had been investigated years ago, and the old-timers still talked about all the missed work, the damaged careers, the accusations, the nightmare of it all.

"According to our records," Muñoz said, "our Frémont DNA is still here, still protected, untouched."

Angall swallowed before she asked the question that was first and foremost on her brain. But in her few-second pause, no one else jumped in with the query, so she felt compelled to speak.

"Did you just check the records?"

Kamel looked at her with a little bit of amusement. Angall closed her eyes for a half second. She probably could have asked that a bit more tactfully.

She had just asked her boss—well, her boss's boss's boss—if she had compared the records to the actual material.

Stott had turned slightly. Apparently that question interested him more than the rest of the conversation had.

"Of course not." Muñoz sounded amused. "I put a team in place, and we all reviewed each other's work. We've been here for days, making certain there is no leak."

"And there isn't?" Kamel asked.

"We're fine," Muñoz said. "No leak, nothing untoward. I documented all of it, and it has already gone to the Inspector General for our division."

"We're off the hook, then." Stott let out a small sigh. "Good. Because I don't ever want to go through an inspection again."

But Angall couldn't let it go. "Then how did the DNA get out there? I thought Frémont was one of those captured DNAs, impossible to get."

"So did I," Muñoz said, "but as I investigated, I discovered three different sales of Frémont DNA decades ago."

"You did?" Stott's face became a weird shade of puce. Apparently, that was what he looked like when he blushed.

"Yes, we got that too, or some samples of it, anyway. It's not as pure as our DNA, which came directly from the man himself when he was in Earth Alliance Prison. The DNA was stored badly or contaminated by something, and could only be used for fast-grow clones, which were pretty erratic, even for fast-grow."

"Then it's not the same," Angall said. "Our DNA is pure, and clearly those clones were pure as well."

"It's not the same," Muñoz said softly, "and what it shows is that there is loose Frémont DNA."

"So the idea that we have all of it is just a myth?" Kamel asked.

"It's not a myth," Muñoz said. "I checked the records for that too. Nothing in our records marks the Frémont DNA as complete. We did not do great containment on it. We contained it *after* we realized what a danger Frémont was, and not before."

"So you think the DNA the clones were made of is *old* DNA?" Stott asked.

"Old DNA" was a particular phrase used in the Special Collections Unit. It meant DNA that might have come from a subject's life before he was a criminal, from old clothes or possessions, locations he lived and worked before he came to the notice of the authorities, locations that might not have appeared in any official record.

"I suspect so," Muñoz said. "We won't know—that's not what we do. But someone will find the source, and then we'll get it."

Angall's stomach had clenched. She had always heard about the difficulties caused by old DNA, but she had never truly understood what that meant before.

It meant lives lost.

She had always thought her job was about money, not about lives. Protecting the DNA prevented identity theft and kept newly bred criminals from gallivanting all over the known universe. She had understood that from the beginning.

She hadn't realized that "gallivanting" was too cavalier a word. Newly bred criminals could steal, or they could murder.

Or they could commit mass murder, just like their original had.

She shuddered.

Stott looked at her.

"It's not your fault," he said. "Stop worrying about it."

As if she could.

She would worry about moments like this for the rest of her career or, more realistically, for the rest of her life.

23

MORE THAN A WEEK AFTER THE EXPLOSION, ONLY A HANDFUL OF ANNIVERSARY Day patients remained in Crater View Hospital. Those that did remain had unexpected medical problems. Some of them had bodies that rejected the nanohealers and probably needed more sophisticated care. Some were going through round after round of treatment to replace skin lost to severe burns.

And many had such traumatic brain injuries that their next of kin would face a serious decision—see if they could repair the brain and end up with a completely different human being than the one who had been injured on Anniversary Day or let their loved one go.

Wilma Goudkins had not found a hotel room yet or even stopped to find a place to stay. The administrator at Crater View saw Goudkins' credentials and allowed her to keep her bags in his office. He knew of channels that helped visitors find places to stay, but at the moment, the entire city was full.

Rescue workers, aid workers, families, hangers-on all crowded into what places were available. The number of hotel rooms was down, and so was the number of the available apartments and homes.

There would be too few, even if emergency personnel hadn't shown up.

A good third of the city had been displaced. The mayor was apparently not paying attention to the price-gouging going on either. So many people had no place to live or stay that some were sleeping in the train station and in other public sites.

The police were so busy with the fallout from the explosions (and each police officer's personal losses) that they weren't ticketing transients either.

Goudkins didn't want to take space away from people who really needed it. She was going to have to find out what had happened to her sister, and then try to get into her sister's apartment. At least the apartment wasn't in the destroyed area; Goudkins had checked that far.

But it was hard to access someone else's place, particularly if no one in the building knew Goudkins. She would need her credentials, her DNA profile, and some kind of proof about her sister's whereabouts.

She might be able to do that last, but she hoped—and there was that word again—that she wouldn't have to bully her way into the apartment by using her status as Earth Alliance Security.

She was already using that status more than she had planned. It had gotten her a ride to the hospital, and it had gotten her directly into the administrator's office.

Carla wasn't listed as a patient, either now or on Anniversary Day, but that didn't mean anything. A number of patients had been injured too badly to identify themselves. Most of their links and personal chips had stopped working when they got injured, which told Goudkins that whoever supplied the chips was probably facing a large lawsuit at some point, because she suspected they had all been purchased from the same place.

Most people did not have DNA on file anywhere but in their own networks, which meant that the hospital had to get a court order to compare the DNA of an unidentified patient without relatives to existing DNA—and then the hospital had to know whose DNA it was so that they could ask for the comparison DNA.

A lot of people went unidentified because of silly regulations, designed to prevent DNA theft and cloning. She supposed identity theft was a serious problem in the settled part of the Alliance, but she thought failing to identify the dead and wounded was a worse problem.

Of course, at the moment, she was biased.

The hospital had been built on the crater's outer shell, actually at what the locals called the Lip of the Rim. Like the Top of the Dome resort, the hospital had been built right against the dome, against all modern regulations but standard at the time of the hospital's construction.

The entire city of Tycho Crater was lucky that Crater View hadn't been destroyed when the Top of the Dome exploded.

The poor and unidentified were brought here—maybe because they were considered expendable. The wealthier patients had gone to Tycho Crater's six other hospitals, all in more protected parts of the city.

Goudkins had checked all the hospitals and the city morgue relentlessly since Anniversary Day, looking for her sister's name or some variation on it. And she hadn't found a Carla Goudkins registered anywhere.

Goudkins was assured by everyone she contacted that, if her sister was unidentified, she would have ended up here.

Goudkins wasn't allowed to enter any patient's room. Instead, once she left the administrator's office, she went to the viewing chamber. Most hospitals had them. The chambers were designed so that friends and family could visit with a very sick patient who needed complete isolation.

Too many diseases—and the wrong kind of cures—could be brought in on a nanofiber, so most of the desperately sick saw their loved ones through the viewing chambers. Some hospitals even disabled links so that all communications went through the chambers.

It didn't matter what kind of hospital this was. Every time Goudkins tried her sister's link, she felt like she was sending a message into the void.

The viewing chambers in this hospital were on its lower level in the central core. The hospital—one of the first built in Tycho Crater—had been set up to maximize views of the Moon, so anything that didn't require a window was either in the middle or in the basement or, as in the case of these chambers, both.

An administration tech went with her, mostly to make sure she didn't hack into their system and steal private information about the various patients. More hospital policy, all of which—Goudkins knew—had been developed after someone had done the crimes others were now prevented from even attempting.

The place the tech brought her to was less a "chamber" than it was a pod. She had to slip sideways through the door. Then she had to click off a dozen waivers before the chair rose out of the center of the floor.

Once the chair rose, she either had to leave the room or sit down.

She sat.

Screens appeared in front of her. Almost all of them showed a patient on a bed, curled, or blinking emptily at the ceiling, or covered in healing cloths. Beside each wrapped or damaged face was a hologram of what the hospital's computers deduced the person had looked like before the injuries.

Height, weight, and clothing were also displayed, as well as other vital information that the medical facilities could figure out.

The hospital had deleted all the male unidentified from the images before Goudkins, but didn't delete any of the women who had had children.

Goudkins had recommended it, worrying that there would be too many, but the tech had said no.

"I'm sure you know, Ms. Goudkins," he had said, "that not everyone tells their families about each detail in their lives."

Goudkins didn't consider a child a detail, but she understood the point. She only saw her sister once per year, if that, and if something had happened that Carla hadn't wanted to talk about, then there was no way Goudkins could have found out that information for herself.

The first images were of the living patients—all shapes and sizes, although none of which fit the profile that Goudkins had of her sister. The living patients moved and breathed and sometimes coughed. The images were streamed into the room, with the other detail placed on a side screen.

When Goudkins rejected those, the next set of images was of the dead.

They were harder to look at.

These people had been severed by the sectioning dome or injured in the escape from the Top of Dome. More than a dozen had been in vehicles that crashed into the dome when it sectioned, and an odd few had died of natural causes in nearby shelters.

There were one hundred people who had died, left a corpse—which, the administrator had told Goudkins gently, was unusual in this particular incident (meaning, she guessed, Anniversary Day)—and didn't in some way match up against the list of the missing.

She had placed her sister on that list immediately, but didn't have any up-to-date information about Carla in regards to weight, height, or even hair color. So Carla existed on the list as a name only, not as a fully realized human being.

Sometimes the guesses made of these corpses from the hospital's recognition program were made based on a single limb. The DNA provided some clues, as did the size of the leg in one instance, and the arm in another.

Goudkins diligently went through the images, maintaining the calm she had used to good effect in her investigative training years ago, trying not to speculate.

Nothing—no one—none of these corpses had been her sister. She was certain of it.

But when she rejected the last group of images, a final screen rose. It asked her if she wanted to contribute DNA to match against any database of the dead.

Her job usually did not allow her to contribute DNA to anything. If Alliance security personnel had their identities stolen, they lost their jobs forever. Not counting all of the havoc the DNA loss could cause.

Normally, she would have opted to say no, but she didn't here. Instead, she asked to see the administrator one more time.

Goudkins would contribute DNA if she could do it under tightly controlled circumstances and if she could run the matches.

She would find her sister.

She had to.

Because she didn't want to contemplate what would happen if she couldn't.

24

THE IMAGES WERE FROZEN ON THE FLOATING SCREEN BETWEEN DESHIN and Pietres's daughter Ethelina. Her eyes were red and her face unnaturally gray.

Jakande stood beside Deshin, his back to Deshin's side, monitoring the room. Jakande clearly didn't trust her—not that he should.

Deshin didn't either.

The screen images caught Deshin's eye: the shop, seemingly empty except that Deshin knew Pietres's body was on the floor; the building's exterior as the clone—Syv—hurried down the broken sidewalk.

Normally, Deshin would have bargained for the images, but this wasn't a normal moment.

Instead, he scanned his database to see if he could find out what had happened to the clone that murdered the mayor of Sverdrup Crater. What Deshin found startled even him.

The clone had been murdered by the crowd—ripped apart after he escaped the bomb blast that he helped initiate.

There was a reason that this part of the Moon had fought against joining the United Domes. These two cities, and some of the mining colonies here at the south pole, had a law all their own, one that barely fit inside the Earth Alliance.

Deshin made sure his expression showed none of his emotions. He met the girl's gaze.

"I've seen enough, thank you," he said, telling her without ordering her to get rid of that screen.

She closed her hand, and the screen shrank, then disappeared, with the movement.

Deshin looked around the room as if he were seeing the storefront for the first time. He wasn't, of course, but she didn't know that.

"Do you need help shutting this down?" he asked, deliberately making assumptions for her.

She raised her chin. "I'm not shutting this down."

"Well, you can't run it alone," Deshin said.

She crossed her arms. "Do you think I'm not capable?"

"Yes," he said simply.

She opened her mouth in shock. Clearly, no one had confronted her like this before.

"It's too complicated and too dangerous. The things you don't know can get you killed. Even your father died doing this work, and he was one of the most careful men I ever knew—

"You have no right to speak of my father," she snapped.

"I have every right." Deshin took a step toward her.

Sir, stay close, Jakande sent.

Deshin ignored that. He had only taken one step toward her. What Jakande didn't know was that one step, taken that way, was more than enough to intimidate someone like the girl.

"I knew your father before you were born. I've done business with your father repeatedly over the years, and I know how hard he worked, and the risks he took, risks he shielded you from. I could have come in here and killed you before you even saw my face."

"You didn't know my father was dead," she said, but her voice shook a little.

Deshin shrugged one shoulder. "So? I could have killed whoever was behind that counter. You're not protected here."

"And you're going to protect me." Sarcasm, the weapon of the weak.

He didn't say that to her. "It's not my job to protect you. It is, however, in my interest to keep this business alive. I propose a trade."

"Money for my father's life work?" The sarcasm gave her voice a strength that her body belied.

"Training, for access to all of your father's records and the security footage from the moment your father opened this store until right now."

She blinked. An errant tear fell down the side of her face, but this time, she didn't brush at it.

"Training?" she asked. "The business would still be mine?"

For the time being, Deshin thought but didn't say. "The business would still be yours."

She let out a snort. "What's in my father's records?"

"I don't know," Deshin said. "But I'm willing to send some of my people to work with you in order to find out."

She stared at him for a long moment, then slowly shook her head. He repressed a sigh. She was stupid after all, if she turned down this offer.

The head-shake grew stronger, and then she laughed. Just once.

"I thought you'd try to steal the business. Or you'd ask for discounts or something. I didn't expect this," she said.

He smiled. "I forgot about the discounts. Add those in as part of the price of training."

She placed both hands on the countertop as if it could hold her up. "You're serious."

"Yes," he said.

"You'd train me? In how to—what? Be a bad guy?"

She was trying to bait him now.

He'd been called much worse. "In dealing with the unsavory characters who make up eighty percent of your father's business."

"You don't want merchandise or anything?"

"Just the information, and the records, and the discounts," Deshin said. "Provided, of course, that you want to continue running this business. If not, we can negotiate a price."

She glanced at Jakande. Deshin couldn't see Jakande's face to see if there was any reaction at all, but Deshin would have wagered there wasn't.

"Would you help me avenge my father?" she asked.

"Against whom?" Deshin asked. "The man who killed him is dead."

"The *clone* who killed him is dead. Clones are owned by people. I want to find out who killed him."

"You know who killed him," Deshin said. "If you're keeping the business for revenge, you're doing it for the wrong reason. Better to take some of the things your father sold, store them, and then hire a mercenary to do your dirty work for you."

"You say that so calmly," she said.

He nodded. "In this business, everyone speaks calmly about a lot of horrible things."

She continued to stare at him, as if she hadn't considered any of this. Maybe she hadn't. In the past month, her entire world had ruptured, and she clearly had no idea how to reassemble it.

Even if she didn't sell Deshin the business, he predicted silently to himself that he would own the business within the year.

"Deal," she said. She started to reach out her hand, and then stopped. "You don't mind if I refuse to shake on it?"

He smiled. "I don't mind at all," he said.

25

THEY SENT GOUDKINS TO THE MORGUE.

It was actually located in a tiny dome just outside Tycho Crater. Early in its history, Tycho Crater had suffered a contagion that went from the aausme through nanobots that were cleaning up human corpses, and then somehow infected human beings. The contagion's source wasn't known immediately, and everything became very Earth medieval, with the dead being stored outside of the dome.

Courageous doctors had worked on the corpses outside the dome, unable to come back in until they knew the source of the disease and its cure.

Their names were on the roads leading through the tunnel that took Goudkins to the morgue, and the name of the organization was on a virtual plaque outside the morgue's building.

While she traveled, Goudkins got the entire history, whether she wanted it or not.

Normally she did, which was why her links activated when she noted unusual architecture or something not generally done in human Earth Alliance cultures. She had forgotten to shut off that feature, and it hadn't activated until now. She was on the Moon, after all, and a lot of what was considered normal for humans had developed here and on Earth.

Apparently, a morgue isolated from a dome wasn't considered normal.

Nothing in her day was considered normal. She shut down the links, flagging her system to remind her, when she reached Armstrong's port, to reactivate that feature.

The morgue itself was all cool lines and windows that had a close-in view of the Moonscape. Jagged rocks crowded against the tiny dome, making it feel as if the morgue were on some distant planet, and she was an early colonizer.

The air had no smell at all, which told her that the environmental systems constantly scrubbed everything to such a high degree that nothing organic could breed here, even if someone wanted it to.

Five minutes after Goudkins entered the morgue, a man emerged from a door in one of the steel-blue center walls.

"Officer Goudkins?" He was short and a little dumpy, the kind of dumpy that would get him kicked out of any Earth Alliance position for being out of shape.

"I'm not on duty here," she said. "Call me Wilma."

He inclined his head toward her. "Wilma. I'm Alfonso."

He didn't offer a last name or his hand. Maybe that was custom here, because of the history of contagion. She did not know.

"I understand you want to contribute DNA to identify a possible relative?" he asked.

"I'm a member of the Earth Alliance security team," she said. "I'm only allowed to use my DNA under very controlled circumstances. I would need to run the comparisons myself."

"With supervision, I hope," he said.

They both knew how easy it would be for an unsupervised someone to mess with the database.

"Yes," she said, "as long as we wipe my information when we're done."

"We can do that," he said. "Follow me."

They went through the door he had come out of, and down a flight of stairs. The temperature was lower here, and the air had a tang of chemicals that she didn't recognize.

Most of the doors off the lower corridor were closed and labeled by the function inside. The stairs went down farther, and, according to the building map that had appeared in the corner of her left eye, led to storage pending notification.

In other words, if her sister were in this morgue, she'd be at least one more level down.

Goudkins glanced that way, then forced her brain away from contemplating what lay below.

Alfonso led her into a room in the back, which had a lot of equipment she couldn't identify, and one thing she could. A quick-look DNA analyzer. The Investigative unit had dozens of those. The results from the analyzer always needed double-checking as it had a small error rate, but if it found a match, that match was usually positive. It was the negatives that sometimes got overturned.

She walked over to it, but didn't touch it. "How do we keep my information separate?"

"We add this." He took a small chip out of a package of chips. "Everything we do goes on that chip and you can take it with you."

"Forgive me for being paranoid, but I'm required to ask: How do I know you're not making extra copies?" Usually she didn't apologize for asking that question, but she felt a little less powerful than usual since she wasn't here on Earth Alliance business.

"I'll let you check the system," he said. "I assume you're familiar with DNA analyzers."

Good assumption and stupid decision. Normally, she would warn him about letting someone else tamper with their machines, but she wasn't going to say anything on this day.

She sank into the chair and grabbed one of the swabs. He put the chip into the machine as she did so.

"Thank you for taking time out of your day to do this," she said.

His gaze met hers. He had deep circles under his eyes.

"I'm not taking time," he said. "Ever since last week, this sort of thing has been a crucial part of my day."

She knew he didn't mean keeping someone's privacy, but helping locate bodies for family members.

"I greatly appreciate it," she said softly.

"I know," he said and ran a hand over his face. "Believe me, I know."

26

BERHANE AND Ó BRÁDAIGH ("CALL ME DONAL, PLEASE") SETTLED IN A coffee shop a few blocks from the train station. Berhane had never been to this coffee shop before, which really wasn't much of a surprise.

She hadn't spent a lot of time in this part of Armstrong. Her father would probably lecture her severely if he found out where she was.

She sighed inwardly. She was a grown woman who worried about what her father would think about her whereabouts. She really had allowed other people to run her life.

She had just been starting to step into her own before her mother died. And then it had been as if Berhane had frozen in time.

"Is this okay?" Ó Brádaigh—*Donal*—asked. "I mean, we can go somewhere else if this place makes you uncomfortable."

She looked at him, trying to figure out what he meant. Was he worried that this place was too cheap for her? That she was the kind of woman who wouldn't be seen in a place like this?

That might've been unfair to him. He might have thought she just didn't like the ambience.

But only a few weeks before, she *would* have worried about being seen in a place like this, because she doubted that her father or Torkild would approve.

She smiled at Ó Brádaigh—*Donal*. Donal. He wanted her to call him Donal.

"This is lovely, thank you."

Lovely was probably an overstatement. The coffee shop was small, with dark wood walls and lovely plants that she couldn't identify hanging from the ceiling. The plants had viney leaves that trailed to the floor, and they probably created a lot of oxygen.

Even so, the place smelled of coffee and chocolate, and because of that, seemed incredibly decadent. The smell probably made the patrons less likely to notice the worn booths or the chipped edges on the tables.

Berhane ordered a chocolate espresso, just because this place smelled so much like one, and Donal raised his dark eyebrows, looking amused.

"You'll never sleep," he said.

She shrugged. "It's the middle of the day. I'm not worried."

She didn't want to tell him that she hadn't slept well since Anniversary Day. It brought back all of the nightmares she'd had since her mother's death.

A serving bot brought their drinks. Donal had ordered a raspberry latte. It arrived, an alarming shade of pink.

"My daughter got me hooked on these," he said as he took his drink off the tray. "She ordered it because it's pink."

"But that's not why you ordered it," Berhane said with a smile.

"Certainly not," he said. "I ordered it because it tastes good. Want a sip?"

She did. Normally she would have said no—such things just weren't done. And the moment that thought crossed her mind, she said, "Sure."

He offered her the glass, then took her espresso off the tray. The espresso was very black.

She took a small sip from the latte. It tasted of raspberries and rich cream and was probably one of the most decadent things she'd tasted in years.

"Wow, yum," she said. "I'll remember that."

"It's why I come here," he said. "These things are deadly, but delicious. Everyone needs something like that in their life."

He put his hand on top of the tray and the tray trilled. He had just paid for their drinks.

"You didn't have to do that," she said.

"Oh, but I did," he said. "I owe you. Fiona *loves* that ring. I have to pry it off her neck every night, and she isn't allowed to wear it outside the house. She hates me for that."

"So you owe me because I made your daughter hate you," Berhane said with a smile.

He laughed. The sound was as deep and rich as the coffee.

"That's what I just said, isn't it?" His eyes twinkled. In that moment, she realized that he was one of the most handsome men she had ever seen. "I think you know what I mean."

The shop was a little too warm. Or maybe she was.

"Yes," she said. "I do know what you mean."

His gaze stayed on hers a moment too long. When was the last time a man had looked at her like that? When anyone had?

She couldn't remember.

Her mother would say that she just wouldn't have noticed, that her thoughts were tied up in Torkild, and that had probably been true.

But Berhane hadn't thought of Torkild as much this last year, except to resent him or dismiss him. It hadn't been working out. She had known that, but she had been unwilling to admit that to herself.

"It's nice to laugh," she said to Donal. "I can't remember the last time."

His smile faded. He looked around the shop. The ten other patrons had been looking at them.

"Yeah," he said. "It almost feels inappropriate."

She remembered that feeling from the days after the first bombing. When someone laughed in public, everyone stared. It seemed like the whole city had agreed that laughing had been banned for at least a month.

And she had been grieving so hard for her mother that she had felt the same way.

"We have to laugh at small things," Berhane said, as much to herself as to him. "We're not alive if we don't."

That gaze of his was deep. She could get lost in those eyes.

What would her mother say? She was searching for a rebound.

And this man wasn't someone to toy with. He had a darling child who would become too attached to anyone in his life.

Berhane didn't want to hurt either of them.

And little Fiona had been the highlight of her Anniversary Day. The *only* highlight. (Unless Berhane counted the break-up with Torkild, which would only benefit her in the long run.)

She took a sip of her espresso. It was good and sweet, with a slightly bitter aftertaste. Somehow the flavor worked.

She made herself focus on Donal, not on the past. She wasn't sure why he wanted to spend time with her, but she wasn't going to ask him either.

Asking would make her seem needy.

"Are you going to try to talk me out of going into the field?" Berhane asked.

He rested his right elbow on the table and put his chin in the palm of his right hand. It was a young, wistful move, making her realize what he must have looked like as a boy.

Dark eyes, incredible intensity, lips that seemed to smile even when he was serious.

"No, I'm not going to talk you out of anything," he said. "I think I understand why you want to go."

She turned her head. He was going to say something patronizing. Torkild would have. Her father too.

Since she was attracted to this man, and it was too soon to be attracted to anyone, she decided to let him disparage her. It would be the best way to make her see him as a real person and not as someone interesting.

"Why do you think I want to go?" she asked.

He let his arm drop. He took the glass of pink liquid and pulled it toward him.

"My wife," he said quietly, not looking at Berhane. "She died in the bombing four years ago."

Berhane's face flushed. Whatever she had expected him to say, it hadn't been that.

"I'm sorry. I didn't know."

"I know you didn't." He grabbed a spoon and stirred the latte. The spoon clinked on the glass. "They didn't…find her…right away, and I kept thinking she would come back to us. Fee was only two months old. I was babysitting her that day. I should have been at work, and Laraba should have been at home. She had leave to stay with Fee. I didn't. But Laraba had some appointment at the medical school—she was a professor there—and I agreed…"

His voice trailed off. He raised his head.

"You don't want to hear this," he said, his voice suddenly normal again.

"I do," Berhane said. She hadn't met anyone who had lost someone in the first bombing.

Well, that wasn't entirely true. She hadn't met anyone who wanted to discuss what they lost.

But the opportunity had fled. He was already shaking his head, clearly embarrassed. "Long story short, it took them three months to identify her."

"By small amounts of DNA found somewhere," Berhane said.

"Yes." His eyes glittered. "Your mother too?"

Berhane nodded. "It took forever. I thought—I hoped—she had run away."

He laughed, only this time, it wasn't the deep-in-the-gut joyful laugh he'd had before, but a bitter laugh of recognition.

"Yeah, me too," he said. "But I couldn't understand how she could leave Fee."

"And you," Berhane said.

He shook his head. "Oh, I can be an asshole, and I wasn't happy that day about missing a morning of work. I could understand how Laraba could leave me. But Fee was her whole world."

Such sadness. Berhane felt drawn to it, and knew she shouldn't.

"It sounds like Fiona is your whole world too." She didn't feel that she had the right to call the little girl "Fee." That seemed like an affectionate, earned nickname.

He smiled, the warmth back in his face. He wasn't looking at Berhane. Instead, he looked to the side, as if he could actually see Fiona.

"She is my whole world," he said. "I didn't think I could raise her without Laraba, but I am. I've managed. And Fee saved my life."

Berhane understood that too, that need to grab onto something. She had made Torkild that something, to his dismay. Maybe the end of the relationship hadn't been all his fault. Maybe Berhane had refused to let him go because she couldn't let anything go after the bombing.

Donal was saying, "I know it seems silly to say that about a two-month old, but really—"

"You had to stay focused on the present," Berhane said. "You didn't have time to grieve."

His gaze was on hers again. She felt an odd jolt, as if he had actually touched her.

"Yes," he said with a kind of wonder. "Exactly."

"Anniversary Day couldn't have been easy for you," Berhane said.

"Oh, God, you have no idea—" He stopped himself and smiled sheepishly at her. "Except that you do."

She nodded. A lump formed in her throat. She made herself take a deep breath, hoping the lump would go away without tears.

"And," he said, as if by way of apology, "your fiancé was an asshole to you just before so you had no one to go to for comfort."

That made Berhane smile. Whatever Torkild was good at—and there were many things (mostly intellectual)—comfort wasn't one of them.

"He came back," she said. "They didn't let the ships leave, and to his credit, he tried to comfort me. The softer emotions aren't in his skill set."

Donal took a sip of that egregiously pink drink, then set it aside.

"Forgive me, but you two didn't look like you belonged together. Even fighting...I mean..." Then he shook his head. "I'm sorry. I'm out of line."

It was her turn to rest an elbow on the table. "No, I want to hear this. No one besides my mother ever talked to me about Torkild."

Donal gave her a surprised look. "No one?"

Berhane shrugged. "I…my close friends, they all went to school or took jobs off-Moon. They kinda thought I was a throwback for staying here."

And of course, she hadn't made many other friends in the last few years. Since her mother died, at least, if not before. There were a few people she had regular conversations with at the university, but she hadn't seen most of them after the bombing.

She hadn't seen anyone for a long time.

He nodded. "Sometimes life just gets in the way, doesn't it?"

"Yeah," she said softly. Then she made herself smile at him. "Which is not going to get you off the hook. Tell me what you saw with me and Torkild."

"Why?" Donal asked.

"I'll tell you later, so I don't taint whatever it is you're going to say."

"Fair enough," he said. "When people in love fight, the passion spills over. Bystanders should be able to look and see the attraction. The fighting should be just as profound as the lovemaking."

Berhane's cheeks heated.

Donal's eyes twinkled. He clearly saw her discomfort.

"However, you were mad. He just stood there, as if you were some off-kilter stranger. He looked at you with a little sadness, but it was that superior sadness some people get when a child is out of control and those people believe that no one should ever let their child behave like that."

That last bit sounded like experience. But Berhane understood it.

"Of course, I might be biased," Donal said. "I like you, and the fact that someone was treating you like that…"

He shrugged and spread his hands in a silent apology.

"And here I am, making an ass of myself," he said.

"No," she said. "No."

She took a deep breath, then extended her hand. The movement felt like such a risk. A tentative touch with someone she didn't know.

"Thank you," she said. "For the honesty. It means—"

He took her hand and stole her breath at the same time. His fingers were warm and dry and callused and somehow electric. They sent a charge through her skin.

She felt like she hadn't been alive until that moment.

The flush on her face grew.

He could probably see her acting like such a school girl, and he was probably thinking she was such an idiot.

"I've got to pick up Fee," he said. His hand was still entwined with hers, so she started to pull away.

He tightened his grip.

"But," he said, as if he knew that she was uncomfortable. *Embarrassed.* "I'd like to do this again. I'd like to spend some real time with you. Is that something…?"

Her father would say that this man, who flat-out told her the day they met that he couldn't afford a ring like the one she was just giving away, was after Berhane for the money. Her mother would have gently suggested an investigation. Torkild would have laughed and said that Berhane had come down in the world.

"I would like that too," Berhane said. "I would like that very much."

Donal grinned. He brought their entwined hands up to his mouth and kissed the knuckle beneath her middle finger. A shiver ran through her.

"Wonderful," he said. "The end of the week, maybe? Dinner?"

Her father would want to know why she was out for dinner, who she was seeing, what her plans were.

She didn't care.

"Yes," she said.

"I'll make plans," he said. "I'll send them to you. Do you have a link I could access…?"

"Yes," she said. "I'll send it, if yours is easy to find."

"It is," he said.

Then mine is too, she sent, using a private link that her father did not have access to. One she hadn't used in a long time, not since her mother was alive.

Berhane wrenched her thoughts away from that.

Wonderful, he sent along those links and smiled. He kissed the knuckle on her thumb, then set her hand down gently, before disentangling.

He stood at the same time. "I'm sorry," he said. "I can't be late for Fee."

"No, you can't," Berhane said. "Go."

"Remember," he said as he headed toward the door. "Dinner!"

"I will," she said, as she thought, *How could I forget?*

27

ALFONSO LET GOUDKINS RUN THE DNA MATCH. HE DIDN'T EVEN LOOK at the screens.

Security, in this lab at least, was frighteningly lax. She was glad that she had decided to follow protocol after all. She couldn't imagine what kind of junk was on the machines and what might have gotten stolen as a result.

After her DNA sample was analyzed, it only took a minute to run the match against the unidentified bodies from Anniversary Day. As she had already guessed, her sister wasn't among them.

Since Alfonso was spending more time leaning against the wall with his arms crossed and his eyes closed than he was supervising Goudkins, she figured she could run one illicit search. He probably wouldn't care. Not that he would notice while he took his micronap.

She ran her DNA against the information listed for the bodies that had already been identified. It took the machine a moment longer to perform that analysis. It wasn't a common request and she'd had to input a few extra queries.

She did it all through holographic keystroke, so that she didn't leave extra DNA on the keyboard he had provided, and so that she didn't wake him with her voice commands.

While the machine compared the data, she scanned the room. Nothing untoward that she could see. Not that it mattered. She had to keep reminding herself that she wasn't working.

Work seemed to be a default for her. She relied on it when she didn't want to think about anything else.

After a moment, the results came back. No matches.

She wasn't surprised, and weirdly, she was a little disappointed. She wanted to know what had happened to Carla, and deep down, she feared she never would.

She wiped the information from that search just like she had done with the previous search. She would need Alfonso's help removing the chip.

"Alfonso?" she said softly, so that she woke him up gently.

"Hmmm?"

"I think I'm done."

He coughed and stopped leaning against the wall, all before he'd opened his eyes. When he did, he looked even more exhausted than he had when he'd fallen asleep standing up.

"Done?" he sounded surprised. Had he not known he had fallen asleep? He needed a few hours off.

But she wasn't going to tell him that.

"Yeah," she said.

"Did you find her?" He managed to have compassion in his voice despite his exhaustion.

"No." She sounded curt, even though she hadn't meant to. It was hard to hide her feelings today. It probably would remain hard for quite a while.

"Have you taken out your chip?" he asked.

"No," she said.

"Let's try one more thing." He walked over to her side, then crouched. It looked like he was going to use the keyboard before he remembered himself and stopped.

"What do you want me to do?" she asked, making sure he couldn't manipulate any of the screens or the data.

"We have a lot of small…" He glanced at her, as if he wasn't sure how to express what he needed to say.

"It's all right," she said. "You won't offend me."

He sighed, as if he didn't believe her. She wasn't sure she believed herself.

"We have, um, a lot of—when the bomb went off…ah, I'm sorry, I don't know how to say this." He ran his hand over his face again, obviously a nervous habit.

She waited for him to finish.

He shot her an apologetic look.

"When…um…the bots come across what's clearly organic material, they collect it, and so do our S&R people."

It took her a moment to realize that S&R was Search & Rescue. Organic material. All these euphemisms. Brain matter. Blood. A bit of skin. Maybe a bone fragment. Things that DNA could be extracted from.

"Bot collection of larger…um…samples? Material?…anyway, um, we can compare to that. It'll be weeks before we can compare to the microscopic…um, bits…but the larger…we can do that now."

She froze at the computer. Did she want to know her sister had been reduced to "organic material"? Goudkins worked to get that phrase out of her mind.

"How do I compare?" she asked.

"I'll walk you through it," he said, and then he did.

28

PEARL BROOKS SAT IN SEMI-DARKNESS, LOST INSIDE NUMBERS. SHE SPENT most of her days dealing with numbers and their implications. Numbers were so much easier to handle than people. Numbers had never done her wrong.

She could trust numbers, if she could find the right equations and the best ways to verify them.

Her office was in the very center of the Currency Division of the Earth Alliance Treasury Starbase. She couldn't count on her office remaining here for long; the Earth Alliance Treasury was always vulnerable to attack, so its location was kept a secret and it remained in one place for two months or until the location was known, whichever was shorter.

It didn't matter where the staff worked. What mattered was where the data was stored, and that changed too. The staff didn't know much about data storage, and anyone who asked was flagged. If that person acted suspiciously in any way, they were summarily dismissed, whether or not they had done anything wrong.

In the Treasury Division, a person was guilty when suspected, and there was no proving innocent. You either toed the line or you didn't.

Brooks didn't care about the line. She knew who she was and what she did, and her confidence in herself, and in the numbers that she loved, had helped her move up the ranks.

She had started as a low-level analyst in the Human Currency Exchange, which handled conversions of all the millions of human currencies into Earth Alliance Credits. Then she got promotions, each time with more responsibility, until she moved to the Joint Unit, where she had to prove herself again.

She hated working with aliens, and had asked to be reassigned. It was one thing to learn numbers. It was another to learn the social behavior of all of her colleagues, some of whom had more appendages than she had strands of hair.

It had overwhelmed her, and interfered with her study of numbers. She loved watching the automatic conversions as a way to stay calm.

Most of the system was automated, but it still needed a living monitor at times, mostly to judge the importance of interactions, and maybe rank a local coup in Gdansk on Earth below an election in Wells City on Mars. Rankings helped determine where the currencies traded and how they would fare against each other as they converted to Earth Alliance Credits.

So beautiful. So elegant. And so simple, despite their seeming complexity.

Because of the numbers and the difficulties she had with some social aspects of her job, she had turned down three different promotions since she had moved into Earth Alliance Currency Division Headquarters.

She could still watch the conversions, and she could overrule anyone below her—the thousands and thousands of employees who thought they knew as much as she did. (They never would; so few of them had the same love of numbers she did, the same comfort with the regimented non-social thinking required in so much of the job.)

She stayed here, mostly so that she could work in silence and follow her passions without any interruption from living beings at all.

Which was what made the message that crossed her division link all the more annoying:

Moon crisis meeting already started. Where are you, Pearl?

She wanted to answer, *here, where the real work is being done,* but she didn't. She sighed. She had hoped they would have forgotten her. She had already submitted her opinion, which she had written with the care of a legal brief. They didn't need her to discuss anything.

Instead of sending her irritated message, she would have to deliver that irritation in person.

Coming, she sent, and stood.

This, *this,* was the reason she hated working with others. They had to have dumb meetings when contact on links or through documents or even vids would work better. But no, someone determined that face-time was important so that everyone would get a chance to respond.

Apparently, some people ignored requests to participate, as they all told her in arch tones. And, she would say in return, sometimes ignoring was the best response.

She got up from her comfortable chair, which she had molded to her entire body and often felt like a second skin, and walked through her holographic screens.

She loved the symbolism of that. It felt like the numbers were part of her, if only for a moment. She left the screens running, their numbers scrolling faster than most people could ever see, and stepped into the hallway.

This particular part of this particular starbase was narrow and dark. Disty-designed for humans, someone had told her, and she believed it. The Disty knew that humans were taller than they were, but they never seemed to realize how much taller.

Fortunately, Brooks was not that tall, and quite thin—not because of enhancements but because (everyone said) she didn't eat enough. She could wend her way through the twisty hallways without bending over (much). What she hated was the dim lights. Even on full, they made everything seem Mars-red and dusty.

The meeting room had been redesigned into a conference room that suited humans. Brooks didn't realize until she got there that this meeting was humans-only.

She should have refused participation on that fact alone.

Of course, everyone was there—all fifty department heads. They looked up at her as if she had done something wrong by being late.

So she leaned just inside the doorway, and crossed her arms.

Since they were all staring at her—a sea of brown and tan faces, resentful eyes, and hair color ranging from white to sea-green—she decided to take control.

"Someone want to tell me why you folks felt it necessary to have a face-to-face without our colleagues from other species?" she snapped. She was laying the baseline for that particular argument.

"We figured we'd present it to them after we had human agreement," Roger Srisati said. Srisati particularly annoyed her. He had frown lines so deep he could funnel sand through them, and he seemed to think he was a gift to finance.

"Present what?" she asked, even though she knew she shouldn't.

"We need to find a legal means to send money to the Moon. The crisis there is severe, and—"

"You're kidding, right?" she snapped. "*That's* what this is about?"

She made it sound like she didn't know, even though she did.

"Not entirely," Veda Puth said. She had auburn hair that she piled on top of her head and let it cascade around her face in waves. "The Moon doesn't have its own currency…"

Yes, I know that, Brooks wanted to say, but she had learned that some sarcastic remarks were simply overkill.

"…and many here believe that the impact on the Earth Alliance credits will continue to be devastating—"

"It hasn't been devastating so far," Brooks said. "I'm actually surprised at how little this crisis has moved the currency markets. I would venture to say it's statistically insignificant."

The phrase *I would venture to say*, she had learned, made it sound like she was participating, when really, she wanted to shake every single person in the room and force them to understand how the damn markets worked. The Moon wasn't the Earth, for God's sake. If every major city on Earth had been targeted, maybe the Earth Alliance credits would have suffered more, particularly since so many Earth Alliance headquarters were located in those major cities.

But the Moon? The Port of Armstrong wasn't even damaged. Nothing was going to affect the currency markets unless the port was rendered unusable.

Puth looked down, clearly rebuked by Brooks's words. One of the other people toward the back, a woman Brooks didn't know, said, "Pearl is right. We don't need to worry about the Earth Alliance financially. The worst is over."

They hoped, Brooks thought but didn't say. If she were prone to biting her lip to remain quiet, she'd have bitten through the damn thing by now, and her part of the meeting had just started.

"What we're doing here, really, is seeing if we can find a way to shave a millionth of a percent off some transactions and designate it into a fund to help the Moon through the crisis."

"That's not legal," Brooks said.

"It is if the Earth Alliance Financial Board agrees," Srisati said.

"Humans and non-humans," Brooks said. "And most non-humans can't give a crap about the Moon. Hell, most humans can't either. You do realize that only one percent of the human population of the Earth Alliance lives inside Earth's solar system, right?"

Half the people in the room were now looking at their hands. How happy everyone must have been that she arrived. She smiled inwardly, her sarcasm amusing her at least.

"It's a stupid idea," she said, "as I told you all in my brief. And, as I mentioned, we all have to vote yes to pull off any kind of charitable gift from the Earth Alliance, which hasn't happened in my lifetime, and I doubt it will. Besides, has anyone thought about who might be the beneficiary? There is no overall Moon government."

Someone started, "The United Domes of the Moon—"

"The United Domes of the Moon," Brooks said, "is a start-up government whose leader was killed on Anniversary Day. The United Domes of the Moon has no standing inside the Earth Alliance, because that leader, in her brilliance, never applied for standing. So we couldn't give them money if we wanted to. So, if you people want to contribute to the recovery of the Moon, by all means do so. There are lots of charitable organizations that would *love* your donations. But stop wasting time talking about something that isn't going to happen."

She stood up, uncrossed her arms, and smoothed her shirt. The entire room stared at her as if they were afraid of her.

And if they were afraid of her, they shouldn't have insisted that she leave her little office-cave for this time-waster.

Oh, that's right: they needed her. For their silly, worthless, unanimous vote.

"The problem with you people," she said into their silence, "is that you don't think. You want to help the Moon? Then go direct. Because what you're trying to do needs some rewritten rules, it needs approval all up the chain of command, and I guarantee that there will be legal challenges."

"How can you guarantee that?" a woman asked.

"Because she'd challenge it," someone else said softly.

Brooks smiled at that person, whose face was lost in the reddish darkness at the back of the stupid conference room.

"That's right," she said. "Because there's all kinds of improprieties going on here, including wasting staff time on frivolous and useless meeting items. My point, though, is valid. Your method will get money to the Moon in ten or fifteen years. If you just fucking donate, you'll get money there next week."

They stared at her. Someone had to have thought they could convince her to share their agenda, but whoever that someone was wasn't speaking up any longer.

"Now," she said, "if you'll all excuse me, I have some real work to do. And next time? Read my brief before paging me. Because none of you people are ever going to change my mind. That would take logic and reason, and you all seem to function on something else entirely."

"Yeah," said a different person in the darker part of the room. "Compassion."

She let out a sigh. That word irritated her to no end.

"Compassion?" she said. "You actually believe you're compassionate? Because more people die every day due to the byzantine laws of the Earth Alliance than ever will in some catastrophe like Anniversary Day. There are wars going on all over the Alliance that our leaders feel are 'local' and therefore must 'run their course.' Refugees have no place to go, particularly if they apply for help from outside the Alliance, in places such as the Frontier. But some big crisis in a mostly human place, something that hits the news and is in our faces because it's the 'center of the Earth Alliance,' and you all believe you need to 'act compassionately.' Bullshit. You wouldn't know compassion if it bit you on the ass."

"That's an unfortunate metaphor," Puth said, and everyone in the room laughed.

Everyone except Brooks. She shook her head.

"We're here to keep the Alliance running," she said. "We have a really important job, even if it seems dry to most of you. Give money if you want to, but don't make it part of our work day, and leave those of us who actually care about our jobs out of it. You won't get me to vote on your stupid projects, so stop asking."

She stalked down the hall, but not fast enough to outrun the comments.

"...told you..."

"...really is an android, I swear..."

"...likes numbers better than people..."

That last was probably true. Because numbers weren't stupid and they followed set rules. Just like the people working in this starbase were supposed to.

Of course they never did.

And they always failed to see the irony in that.

She was acutely aware of that irony. She faced it every single day. Irony was one of the few things that kept logical people sane in the Earth Alliance.

Because if someone inside the Alliance didn't have a deep appreciation for irony, she would go crazy in a matter of weeks.

Brooks didn't like crazy. And she didn't like harebrained. And she really didn't like her colleagues.

She returned to her office and its floating screens, the numbers scrolling, whispering to her, and—yes—comforting her, as only the best things in life could.

29

THERE IT WAS, ON THE FLOATING SCREEN IN FRONT OF HER.

Familial match. Sisters.

Followed by a number that predicted accuracy—something in the quadrillions to one that the match was wrong.

Goudkins swallowed hard as she stared at it, her brain stuttering. She was supposed to do something, but she didn't know what it was.

She didn't want to ask Alfonso, who hadn't given her his last name. She didn't even want to look at him.

Instead, she stared at the screen floating in that tiny room in the Tycho Crater morgue. The information in front of her morphed into two screens.

Possible image of the deceased based on DNA profile. Some information, such as weight, scars, and the like, might be variable...

And then her sister Carla's face appeared, proportions off—the image wasn't sharp enough. Carla had cheekbones that looked like they could cut glass. The eyes were wrong too. They were flat, unrealistic.

Carla's eyes were alive and snapping with intelligence.

Carla's eyes were alive...

Goudkins made a small sound in the back of her throat and pushed her chair back. Tears threatened, and that embarrassed the hell out of her.

She didn't cry. She never cried. She hated people who cried in front of professionals. Crying was for moments alone, so that no one saw how deeply someone was hurt or moved or saddened.

Or grieving.

"How…" her voice broke, and she willed it to stop. "I mean, where was this sample found?"

She couldn't use the phrase "organic material." That little bit was her sister.

Some bot had found her sister somewhere. Maybe a drop of blood, maybe something that showed she wasn't dead after all, just hurt, and Goudkins could continue to look for her, maybe in the hospitals, maybe in Carla's apartment…

"Um." He leaned across her and let his hand rest above the keyboard. "May I?"

"Just tell me how to do it," she said.

He told her where the information was—under some code, in the back of some section, on some map she hadn't even realized was there.

A tiny red dot appeared in a blackened area of the map. The blackened area was right in the center of the two-dimensional image of Tycho Crater.

She didn't have to guess where that was, but she still wanted him to tell her.

"I'm sorry," he said softly, and she could tell he'd done this before. Countless times before. A few minutes ago, she had felt compassion for him, doing this day in and day out as his job.

Right now, she just wanted him to get it over with.

"This is the rubble of Top of the Dome. I can find exactly what they took it off of."

"So she could have gotten out," Goudkins said, "and this was just left behind from an injury?"

She hated the hope in her voice.

"Um." He sounded doubtful. "You can go deeper in the map, see if there is some matching material nearby."

Material. That word again. She hated it too.

She followed his instruction at going deeper. Little yellow dots appeared on the enlarged map section to show where more of the "organic material" had been found.

There were a lot of yellow dots.

"I can ask it to do a probability search of whether or not this was a wound or something more…dire," he said.

"Yes," she said. She needed it. She needed the confirmation. She needed to know.

That was why she was in the morgue in the first place.

He had her input a few commands, and the probability search was done: 99.9999%.

Something dire, in his words.

In the words of the program, 99.9999% certainty that the subject was deceased.

Goudkins closed her eyes. She wasn't the kind of woman who held on to small probabilities. And she'd worked with these kinds of devices and programs before.

The machines never ever stated that they were 100% accurate. But the more accurate the program believed it was, the more nines it added to the right side of the decimal point.

If she were back at Earth Alliance Security Headquarters, she wouldn't tell anyone about the slim possibility of error. She would look at that number as a guarantee. These samples had come from a deceased person.

Her sister Carla had died on Anniversary Day.

In the Top of the Dome.

Because she went back in, thinking that was what Goudkins would do. Dammit.

"Thank you," she said to Alfonso. She stood up, her knees shaking.

"You want the chip, right?" he said.

Crap, she would have left it. All that caution, and she would have left her own DNA behind. He was helping her.

She had to focus.

"Yes, sorry," she said. She leaned forward and removed it herself, just like he had instructed her to.

Then she wiped the system's memory, which she knew how to do from her work in Earth Alliance Security.

She pocketed the chip.

"Thank you," she said, standing upright. "You've been very helpful. More than I can say."

He bit his lower lip. "I'm sorry."

"It's all right," she lied. And forced herself to concentrate again.

He watched her, clearly uncertain what she was going to do next.

"Can you give me something? A document, something, so that I can get into her apartment tonight as next of kin?"

"Yeah," he said. "I'll issue a certificate. It'll only take a few minutes. Do you mind waiting here?"

Mind. Waiting. She put the words together, hating how sluggish her thoughts had become.

"No, I don't mind," she said.

He left the room, and she was alone.

Truly alone.

Those relatives she had, the ones she never saw, were all she had left. The person who had known her all her life was gone. Just gone.

Vaporized.

That was a much better word than the phrase "blown to bits." But her sister had been blown to bits. A recovery bot had found the bits and Goudkins had just used them to identify Carla.

Or what was left of her.

She put the heel of her hand against her forehead.

The hope was gone. Completely gone. And that made her feel as if she had nothing to hold on to.

This place—this city—was such a mess that she wasn't even certain she could hold a funeral. And how would she handle the estate? Did Carla even have an estate? Did it go to Goudkins?

She was making assumptions that she had no right to make.

God, death was full of decisions. She remembered that from her parents' deaths.

But Carla had handled most of that.

Leaving Goudkins to do her job and live her life.

Just like she had done now.

Goudkins could walk away, and no one would know except, maybe, this guy named Alfonso-something, who needed sleep more than Goudkins did.

But she wasn't going to walk away.

She had a final obligation to her sister, and she would do it. Whatever it took.

ONE MONTH
AFTER ANNIVERSARY DAY

30

ARMSTRONG SEARCH & RESCUE SENT BERHANE TO LITTROW. SHE HAD requested time in one of the more distant domes, maybe Glenn Station or even Yutu, but Kaspian had vetoed that. He still believed that she would work for a day and quit.

He told her that she had to put in at least a week of hard work near Armstrong before he ever sent her far from her home.

She was determined to impress him.

Which, she realized when she arrived at the bomb site, would be very hard to do.

She was with a team of a dozen workers. They had been cautioned that they could only work in areas that had already been cleared by investigation teams. Very few areas had been cleared, because there weren't enough investigators.

But the investigators had gone to the original bomb sites first—or what they assumed were the original bomb sites. In Littrow, that meant they went to the place where the governor's mansion had been. From the footage that the investigators had from before the bombing, they believed (although they did not see) that the bomb had been placed there.

They were still working on the area, but they had cleared parts of it.

Berhane had no idea what exactly they were doing, or how they could clear a site, but hers wasn't to question. Hers was to go in and work.

Even though everyone knew there was no rescue involved, Armstrong Search & Rescue, along with the other S&R organizations, was the only one that had the equipment to do the recovery work needed to find the bodies—or what was left of them.

It was grim work, or so Kaspian had warned her, as if telling her that would change her mind. It wasn't going to change anything, except maybe her point of view about her own self-worth and importance in the world. She fully expected a reminder of how unimportant she truly was.

The environmental suit she was assigned would be hers until she decided she no longer wanted to be part of Armstrong S&R. She offered to bring her own suit, but Kaspian had turned that down.

If we let you do it, we let everyone do it, he said. *And not everyone can afford a top-of-the-line environmental suit designed for harsh environments. And don't misunderstand this: you'll be going into one of the harshest environments on the Moon.*

That hadn't scared her off. Nothing had scared her off. In fact, it had strengthened her resolve tremendously.

The train ride from Armstrong took only half an hour. That was why Littrow had been chosen as the center of the new government in the first place. The other domes had complained that Armstrong would be too powerful if the center of the United Domes had been there, but everyone knew how important it was for government officials to be close to the port.

Littrow had been a compromise.

Not twenty years ago, it had been one of the smallest domes on the Moon, but opportunists, like her father, saw how the debate about the United Domes was going, and built up all kinds of housing and shopping districts near the city center, anticipating a lot of growth once the government site had been chosen.

The speculation worked—her father's speculation almost always worked—and now those buildings were in ruins.

He saw profit in rebuilding them.

She saw lost lives.

An official with Littrow S&R met their group at the train station and carted them to the edge of the segmented dome. Littrow S&R hadn't really existed two weeks ago, except as an outline of an organization, something the town had known it needed.

Now, it was composed of volunteers who, Berhane suspected, were as conflicted about what had happened to their city as she had been back when her mother died. They really couldn't work—they hadn't had any training and they had no equipment—so they mostly organized and co-ordinated with Armstrong S&R. They also sent quite a few members to Armstrong for training.

She suspected that by the end of the month, Littrow S&R would become large enough to handle some of its own recovery work.

The official led them to the approved area. It was on the far side of the sectioned dome, in front of what had been the center of Littrow. It was hard to see the damage through the section. Fine shrapnel from the bomb had hit the clear material so hard that it looked like the bottom part of the section had been painted black. The spray went upwards, thick in the middle and fine at the top. Through the top part, black chunks, rocks, and parts of buildings were barely visible.

Within hours, Littrow had capped the hole in the dome and turned the gravity back on, but had left the rest of the environmental systems off inside. All of the domes had done that, so that the Earth Alliance (and other) investigation teams would be able to work on a relatively untouched site.

Some of the domed communities, with more money and a better S&R organization than Littrow's, had actually scraped the exterior of their domes and searched the land outside it for materials that had been blown out with the top of the dome.

Littrow hadn't done that. Someone in the remaining local government had ordered the dome cleaning units to turn on, and any material that had escaped the dome's original confines was gone forever.

That made her sad.

The dozen Armstrong S&R workers had a private link that was secure and encoded. No one wanted the locals to hear about a found but unattached body part, or to hear the reactions of the searchers as they discovered something more gruesome than ordinary.

In addition to signing all the waivers, Berhane had had to go through a two-day class in recovery work. (Had she been doing rescue work, she would have needed an even longer prep.) The class included procedures for handling remains as well as codes to use on the links, so that most things went undescribed.

She had loaded the codes into her AutoLearn program and replayed it over and over again, as well as storing them (and the procedural reminders) in a chip that she could access while she worked.

She didn't want to make any mistakes.

She was responsible for five bots. They would be linked to her so that she would control their movements. Mostly she didn't have to tell them what to do; the links were so that she could stop them if need be. One debris platform would be assigned to her as well, and it was actually marked with her identification code.

When the platform was full, she was done, at least until it emptied itself off and then returned for more. Her breaks would come every two hours or when the platform was full, whichever was sooner.

Some of what she had frustrated her. There were DNA sensing devices, things that would help her scrape off the smallest amount of DNA from any debris, but the organization had limited numbers of those tools and wanted them in the hands of the more experienced staff and volunteers. She understood that, but she also knew that relying on the bots to tell her how much human or alien DNA a bit of debris had was a bit like using a hammer as the only tool.

But, as Kaspian told her, they had to limit themselves somewhere. When she protested, he reminded her that nothing would get thrown away. Everything in the debris fields outside the domes would probably be reassessed before being recycled or disposed of.

She tried to ignore all the qualifiers that he used, and hoped he was right.

But she couldn't think about that. Just the amount of debris she could see through the sectioned dome overwhelmed her. She mentally tried to multiply the destruction by 19 domes, and her mind shied away from the amount of work and effort it would take to recover anything.

She attached the suit's hood, which sealed around her face, doubling as a clear helmet, then followed her team leader into the open door through the section. Each volunteer went in by herself, her bots and platform following behind.

Just to get into the dome took fifteen minutes. Each volunteer had to pay attention to the route they took, because they would most likely leave on their own for breaks. It rarely took two hours to fill one of the platforms.

That fact alone had broken her heart.

She was one of the last people through the door. The volunteer from Littrow S&R closed the door behind her.

Debris towered around her: spindly stalks of metal, thick rock, and dust—more dust than she had expected. She was glad she wore the environmental suit, just because of the dust.

It wasn't gray like Moon dust. The dust in this section of the dome was mostly black. The governor's mansion had been a stunning building, made from the regolith of the Taurus Mountains. She had been inside it several times, usually at some event on her father's arm.

The exterior of the building had been very gothic, rising above the rest of the city like a beacon, but the interior had been beautiful. It incorporated material from every corner of the Moon, and it had décor from most of the Moon's strongest companies. Celia Alfreda, the governor-general, loved to brag that nothing in the mansion had come from off-Moon: not the materials, not the product itself, not even something as small as a thread.

And now, Berhane walked through the remains of it all.

In some ways, she felt glad that Celia Alfreda had not lived to see this—the symbol of the fledging United Domes government, destroyed so thoroughly. The loss of it, and of the governor-general, made Berhane's heart twist.

So she focused on where she put her booted feet.

The path the crew walked along had been carefully carved from the rubble. It went all the way down to the road or sidewalk or whatever was beneath. There were cracks along the road's surface, probably from the impact of all this weight so quickly, but at least she knew she wasn't destroying evidence.

Someone else—the investigators, most likely—had cleared the way to the mansion site.

She hoped they had done so with care. But considering what she had seen from the investigation of the Armstrong bombing, she doubted that had happened. She suspected all of the rubble alongside of her had once been on this path.

The path was wide and straight. The bots that accompanied her could now flank her. Four did, two on each side. But one bot and her platform remained behind her.

The walk was a cautious one, and since she was last, she wasn't certain if that was because the other new people on the team were having trouble picking their way forward or if it was because this was the preferred method of walking through such hazards.

She knew she had to be careful to keep her suit intact. She could cut it on things and it would self-seal, but too many self-seals and the suit would be compromised.

That was one of the many reasons why Armstrong S&R wanted the volunteers to use S&R's suits. Those at least had been inspected, to make certain there were no flaws. The last thing S&R wanted was for someone to die while doing recovery work.

The bots were programmed to keep her from sharp objects as well. She knew that without being told. There was no other reason for them to flank her like that.

The team finally reached the approved area. They were still several meters from the mansion site. Now she understood how the investigators knew where the bomb had gone off.

Instead of a spectacular building that rose above a well-built cityscape, there was a deep crater. Bits of the building itself had toppled into the crater, but mostly, the crater stood alone, black and shiny and smoother than she expected.

She stared at it for the longest moment, feeling a bit of dislocation. One moment the building she remembered had stood here; the next, this had formed.

No one had told her the power of that bomb—or if, indeed, it had been just one bomb—but her eyes told her that the bomb had been a lot bigger than the one used in Armstrong four years ago. She hadn't seen a crater like this where her mother died. There had been a crater, but it had been shallow and wider spread.

Not deep, as if the Moon's defenses had shut off and an asteroid had hit.

The team leader gave them all a few minutes to stare. Then he led them to their cleanup locations.

Berhane's was to her left, just a meter or so off the main path. A smaller path had been formed, wide enough for the bots and probably some of the equipment the investigators used.

Her stomach flopped.

Time to dig in, one bit of rubble at a time.

She examined the pile she was to pull apart. It was as tall as she was, and the debris seemed to be at most a meter long. She had a new special chip, hooked up to her links by S&R, to examine a pile like that and see where its structural weaknesses were.

The bot beside her would also watch for any possible accident.

She sighed heavily, the sound echoing in her suit's helmet, and ran the chip. It gave her three different suggestions as to where to start, with a recommendation as to which one seemed the safest.

She didn't care which one was the safest. Her eye had caught what looked like a bit of fabric, and she would work her way to that first.

Tentatively, she put her gloved fingers into the pile. It shifted slightly and she quickly pulled her hand away.

You are safe, sent an automated voice on her links. She assumed that was the bot. They didn't really have the capacity to think or reason, but they could do simple tasks and communicate through preprogrammed sentences on links if need be.

She thanked it even though she didn't need to, and put her fingers into the pile again. The gloves had sensors that worked rather like skin and fingertips. She felt the shape of everything, and a suggested texture reached her as well. It wasn't always accurate. Her eyes told her that she was touching smooth metal while the sensor made it feel like smooth wood, but it was close enough.

The bot changed its top to a flat surface, preparing itself to receive some of the debris.

She pulled out some sticks near the cloth. They were round and broken on the edges. She had no idea what they had been. She placed them on the bot, and then continued to dig.

The work was hard, but necessary. And tomorrow, she would move to some other pile. So would the rest of the team.

The rubble spread out before her, and she thought about her father's plans, his *company's* plans (*her* company's plans), which were already underway.

There was a time limit on the search and recovery effort. The time limit varied from community to community, but it was real.

At some point, large machines would come into this part of the dome, remove all the debris to the outskirts of the dome, and then other large machines would sort it.

DNA would be lost.

Hell, actual bodies and body parts (*organic matter* as the S&R teams called them when dealing with donors) would be lost. People would never know what had happened to their loved ones.

She couldn't fight her father—she didn't have the clout in the company—but on some level, she knew he was right. At some point, the dome's interior—all of the domes' interiors—would have to be rebuilt.

She pulled something out of the debris. The long, thin, stick-like thing was soft. The ragged edge had sinew curling from the bottom. A finger, maybe. Human? She couldn't tell.

But it was organic matter.

She'd had enough training so that she didn't fling it away in disgust, like she had done in her early sessions. Now she called a bot over and placed the finger on it, with the linked instruction:

Organic matter. Please treat gingerly.

Then she slowed down as she went through the pile.

Because where there was one body part, she had learned through sad effort, there would be more.

31

DESHIN LEANED AGAINST THE WINDOW OF HIS SHUTTLE, FEELING UNSETTLED. Up ahead, Armstrong's dome glittered in the sun, unbroken and perfect. His heart lifted.

He was heading home.

But he was also aware of how unusual it was to see an intact dome. Flying over the moonscape made him both angry and sad. Damaged dome after damaged dome greeted him, each with a hole somewhere, and bits littered across the ground.

Sometimes those holes were just black spaces in the distance, surrounded by rings of light. Sometimes they looked like a giant inside the dome had punched his fist through the top in a fit of anger.

He had stopped in five damaged domes, as well as several smaller undamaged domes. He was tracing the zoodeh and explosives providers.

The zoodeh suppliers had all ended up like Pietres—dead a week or two ahead of Anniversary Day. Most had died from zoodeh contamination, but many had died in other ways. Some had been stabbed, some had had their heads bashed in. None of the deaths were being investigated by the authorities, as far as he could tell.

He wasn't sure how to figure that out exactly: he didn't want to bring his association with these suppliers into the open.

He leaned back in his chair. The interior of the shuttle was made for comfort—large chairs, entertainment screens for moments that the networks were off-line, food available with the wave of a finger over a holographic screen.

But he hadn't taken advantage of the comfort on this trip. For once in his life, he felt vaguely guilty for all he had, rather than inordinately proud of how he had earned each bit of it.

His security team seemed subdued as well. Jakande sat across from him, also staring at the moonscape. Some of the other team members were playing some kind of holographic game in the back. Usually they punctuated that game with shouts and belly laughs, but on this day—this last month, really—they'd been unusually quiet.

The murders bothered him—not just because they were a clear cover-up, but because they had been so unnecessary.

The suppliers he knew wouldn't have mentioned the name or the appearance of their customers. In fact, Pietres had been unusual in even having a surveillance system that stored images.

There had been no reason to kill these people.

Many of them would have died on Anniversary Day. Deshin might have seen some logic in killing the ones in the domes that weren't targeted, but upon closer examination, even that made no real sense.

These suppliers had aided killers and assassins for decades. Even with attacks as large as Anniversary Day, the suppliers would never have run to the authorities with information. If anything, the suppliers would have deleted what information they had stored, just so that they could plead ignorance and not get charged as an accessory.

The clones had known who to go to in order to get the zoodeh. That meant they knew—or someone knew—that the suppliers wouldn't talk.

Logically, then, the murders were for a different reason.

And the only reason Deshin could think of, the reason he couldn't shake, was for the sheer pleasure of killing. These men knew they were going to commit murder in a week, and then compound it with mass murder, and they couldn't restrain themselves.

They had killed ahead of time just for the joy of it.

Deshin had known a lot of people like that. He'd fired quite a few from his organization. People who killed for the sheer pleasure of it were uncontrollable. Ultimately, they would have made a mistake that would have harmed him or his family or his business.

He always thought they were too dangerous to have around.

"We're not too far out, sir," Jakande said. "Did you want to stop near the construction site?"

There were three different construction sites outside of Armstrong's dome, but only one that did not have some aspect of Deshin Enterprises in it. He'd stopped at a couple of those sites on this trip, as well as several mining operations.

They were the only places that had a lot of easily accessible explosives.

What Deshin had learned at those places had disturbed him almost as much as the murders had.

"No," he said. "Let's just go home."

Jakande nodded, then glanced at the cockpit. He was probably relaying the information to the pilots at that moment.

Deshin looked at the moonscape, at the glittering dome looming ahead of him.

He had been handicapped in his investigations of the explosives that destroyed the domes. He didn't know what the clones or their accomplices had used to blow holes in everything.

With the assassinations of the various authorities, Deshin had known immediately what happened. A zoodeh death had its own signature.

Generally, bombs did too.

But the bombs inside the various domes had gone off in different parts of those domes. The bombs also seemed to have different explosive effects, depending on location.

Some bombs seemed more powerful than necessary, while others weren't strong enough. That was one reason that only twelve of the nineteen domes to suffer explosions had actual breaches of the dome.

He didn't know if the difference was because of the amount of material used, the inexperience of the bombers, or because of location. And he didn't know if the same material was used in each place.

Which made investigating the bombings harder.

The clones had used locals to supply the zoodeh; Deshin figured the clones had used locals to supply the bombs. Over the past few years, however, access to explosives had become highly regulated. No one wanted to have their dome breached like Armstrong's had been breached four years ago.

So the regulations required signature after signature, identification processes involving background checks, DNA investigations, and delayed delivery of the materials. Plus, each user had to guarantee that the explosive material would be used for a specific job, and in some of the domes, spot inspectors had double-checked to make certain the users had done what they said they would.

The only place to find unregulated explosives on the Moon were the unincorporated areas between the domes. The mines owned by corporations, the new building developments outside of the domes, places like that.

And even those places generally followed regulations on explosives—primarily because they couldn't easily purchase the explosive material outside of the domes, where they would be on record.

Still, not every place used explosive material from inside the domes. Some of the shadier operations had private landing strips. These were generally far from Armstrong, some near the south pole, and Deshin had checked those.

And he couldn't get them out of his mind.

Because they'd all lost explosive material, sometimes in large quantities, and sometimes in small. They told him something he had known from his own businesses: explosive theft was common.

He'd actually gone to regulated explosives because they were less likely to be stolen. And he'd put major protections in place at any operation that needed explosives.

He had also tried to phase out explosives in as many businesses as possible, taking the longer, harder, and more costly route of having nanobots disassemble things at the cellular level—or was it the subatomic level? God, he didn't know, although Paavo would. Down to its smallest parts.

Deshin had been doing the math the entire trip back to Armstrong—not for zoodeh this time. The math for zoodeh had led him on this trip.

No, the math he'd been doing was for the explosives.

And even if his estimates were high for the amount of explosives that destroyed the domes on Anniversary Day, he still came out with a number that unnerved him.

Fifteen times the explosives used to destroy all the domes on Anniversary Day were still missing. Fifteen times the destructive power, missing and unused.

And most of it, to his surprise, had gone missing—not two weeks before Anniversary Day, or even the month before. But five years before. Before the Armstrong bombings. Before any inkling that these attacks would happen.

Five years, and many, many, many metric tons of missing explosives.

He wasn't sure he could chalk that up to simple theft.

He needed to find out what had exploded the domes, and then track it by type.

He had a large network of employees, investigators, and security.

It was time to put them to use.

32

BERHANE WAS LATE FOR DINNER—AGAIN. SHE SHOULD HAVE CANCELED, but Donal so rarely got nights free. He was working as hard as she was—harder really, because he had a regular job (some engineering thing that she didn't entirely understand) and he had to parent Fiona full time. He still found two days per week to volunteer for Search & Rescue, although he usually did in-house stuff because he didn't want to put himself in any danger. As he said, he had Fiona to consider.

Finding time to spend with Berhane alone was nearly impossible for him, yet he was making an hour here or an hour there.

Their relationship had progressed beyond the coffee, past the first few dinners, and into the first stages of something physical, but they hadn't had sex yet. They would, she knew, as soon as she finished moving into her new apartment. They certainly couldn't do anything at his house: As he said, he didn't want to give Fiona hope that the relationship would be something more than it actually was.

Berhane hadn't even seen Fiona since Anniversary Day. Berhane suspected Donal would want Fiona to know that he and Berhane were involved when he felt like the relationship had some permanence.

And on days like today, Berhane wasn't sure what permanence was.

She had come directly from the Littrow site. She was exhausted. She had taken two showers—one at Armstrong's S&R facility when she removed the last of her environmental suit, and the other at her father's house before she set out to the restaurant.

It hadn't felt like enough.

She wasn't even sure she could eat.

Beneath that debris pile, she had found parts of at least five people. At least.

Not for the first time, she was relieved she had had an environmental suit on. Not because she didn't want to touch the remains, but because the smell—in an oxygen rich environment—would have been overwhelming.

She had no idea how her counterparts did this kind of work on Earth.

It was discouraging, debilitating, and necessary.

She stopped just outside the restaurant door, giving herself a moment. She wore one of her favorite dresses—a white chiffon thing that billowed around her when she moved. She had put on just enough makeup to feel pretty—or what she would have normally felt as pretty—but today it just made her feel like an imposter.

She felt like she had put lipstick on over sweat and dust.

Still, she knew Donal was inside. He had sent her a message when he arrived, and she had asked him to order since she would be a few minutes late.

She smoothed the soft material of her skirt, took a deep breath, and entered.

The restaurant smelled faintly of garlic, red wine, and coffee. Large flower displays near the entrance added some perfume to the mix. The restaurant was an Earth chain, and didn't have any human greeters at the door.

She didn't mind. She had had her fill of "impressive" restaurants, with each detail laid out. She had left those behind when she tossed Torkild's ring across the departure lounge.

Donal sat near one of the windows, his chin resting on his fist as he looked out onto the street. An appetizer of fried gyoza steamed on a plate in front of him.

"Sorry I'm late," Berhane said as she sat across from him.

He turned toward her and smiled. That smile made her heart jump every single time. She couldn't ever remember feeling that particular emotion before she met him.

"The appetizer just got here," he said. It wasn't a complaint about her tardiness, nor was it a criticism. Just a fact.

She liked that about him too.

"We probably shouldn't schedule on days when you volunteer," he said.

"Then we wouldn't see each other," she said.

She slid a plate toward her and picked up chopsticks. They felt big and clunky in her fingers. Even her hands were tired.

He nodded. "You just look so exhausted."

"It's emotional," she said, although she was certain she was physically exhausted as well. "Our team found—well—"

She didn't want to tell him exactly what they had found.

"I don't mind hearing," he said.

"Oh, it's not dinnertime conversation," she said. "We did find DNA of at least fifty people."

"Excellent," he said.

"It's not," she said. "At least a million are dead, and so many more missing. We didn't even make a blip."

"You helped fifty families," he said softly. "That's more than a blip. It's the world to them. You know it."

She did know it. She just got overwhelmed. So much rubble. So many missing people. So much to do.

He was watching her closely. He hadn't picked up his chopsticks.

"Come on," she said. "Let's eat."

She took two dumplings off the appetizer plate and poured some sauce on them. She made herself take a bite, getting a hit of ginger, onion, and garlic with the soy sauce.

Her stomach rumbled. She had been hungry. She just hadn't realized it.

"I ordered a lot of food," he said, "so go slow."

It was as if he could read her mind. He actually cared about her.

"Tell me about your day," she said. "Tell me about Fiona."

He did. He told some cute story about a dance recital for four-year-olds, about what it was like, negotiating his way through tutus and ballet slippers and tiaras.

He had Berhane laughing by the time the second entrée arrived.

They talked and flirted and laughed and enjoyed.

And as they waited for the baobing he'd ordered with a side of strawberries, he leaned forward.

"Now," he said. "Tell me about your day."

She shook her head. "You know what happened out there. You've been through it."

"You've done it before too. Each day is hard, but today seems to have upset you even more than the others."

He was astute about her. No one had been for four years. It still startled her.

"It's been a month," she said. "The investigations are continuing, as best they can, but there's so much to do. And people like my father want to rebuild right away."

"I know that disturbs you," Donal said. "But the problems inside the shattered domes right now are serious, even with the temporary tops in place. For example, every environmental system has to be routed around. The domes weren't designed for the problems we're facing."

She looked at him, feeling a bit disoriented. What had he just said? This was a side of Donal she hadn't seen before.

"I'm a structural engineer," he said. "I told you before. That's my training."

One of the serving trays tipped the bowls of baobing onto their table. The shaved ice had sounded so good earlier, and now it seemed decadent. The strawberries glistened on top, the richness of the food showing just how lucky Armstrong had been to have been spared on Anniversary Day.

"I'm not agreeing with your father," Donal said. "I am saying that the attackers caused a lot of problems, and not all of them are visible or obvious to most people."

She nodded. She understood that. And she was beginning to understand how much her father's callousness affected her. The last thing she wanted was Donal to be like him. She'd had that kind of relationship before; she didn't want another.

"We were talking about how you felt," Donal said. "I interrupted."

"No, you didn't," she said. "You're right. Life moves forward whether you want it to or not. You and I both learned that four years ago."

"But…?" he said.

"I just wish that we had more money and more help, and the ability to focus, not just on the organic material we find, but on a true DNA search, so we can help the families of the missing. They're going to be hoping forever, and we can't do anything about that, not at this pace."

Donal frowned. "What would you do? We have to rebuild."

"We do," she said. "And it's not the mission of Search & Rescue to continue past the initial crisis. I know. I read the charter."

She wanted to add *have you?* but stopped herself. She realized in that moment how charged she had become.

"Everything will shut down and debris will pile up and someday some future generation will bury it or something or people like my father will recycle it, and on it will be—"

"DNA from the dead," Donal said softly.

Berhane nodded. "It bothers me so much I can hardly sleep."

"So why don't you do something about it?" Donal asked.

She snorted. "I *am*. I volunteered."

"No," he said. "Your father is one of the richest men in Armstrong. Have him fund a foundation or something as part of the charitable work his company prides itself on, to do the recovery of the dead."

"I already asked," she said. "He laughed and said I needed to get over Mother at some point in my life."

Donal closed his eyes, his cheeks reddening. He took a deep breath, then nodded. She'd never seen him quite so upset about anything.

"Your father's a real treat," Donal said after a moment.

She shrugged. "He is who he is. He'll never fund something like that."

"Can you fundraise?" Donal asked. "There have to be a lot of people with money that you've interacted with who would be willing to fund something like this."

Halfway through his comments, her stomach flipped over.

People with money.

She never thought of herself as someone with money. It had been her parents' money, and then it was her father's money.

But she had inherited from her mother, and she also had her own trust. She had more money than she could ever spend. She had said that a million times.

She had the money. Maybe not the capital she would need to run a company that would search for all of the dead on the Moon, but she would have enough to start something that could handle Littrow.

Or start something that would then encourage others to invest.

Because Donal was right. She knew people with money. She knew non-humans with money, and all the heads of the charitable giving arms of the major corporations that operated in Earth's solar system.

She could raise charitable funds. She'd done it before. She even knew who to hire to help her and how to go about it.

"Donal," she said, "you're a genius."

"I am?" he asked.

She nodded, and smiled.

"We're going to make a difference," she said. "We're going to help families, and help the Moon itself heal."

He took her hand. She loved his touch.

"Tell me how," he said.

So she did.

The thrilling adventure continues with the fourth book in the Anniversary Day Saga, *The Peyti Crisis.*

The Moon barely survived the devastation of Anniversary Day. The second round of attacks planned to kill millions more. With the life of every human and alien on the Moon hanging in the balance, the Moon's chief security officer, Noelle DeRicci, races to discover the identity of the masterminds behind the attacks before it's too late.

Desperate to find answers, DeRicci turns to Retrieval Artist Miles Flint and Detective Bartholomew Nyquist for the kind of help only Flint and Nyquist can provide.

A gripping look at a society on edge.

Turn the page for the first chapter of *The Peyti Crisis.*

FIFTY-FIVE YEARS AGO

1

THE VOICE ON HER LINKS, SO FAINT SHE ALMOST DIDN'T HEAR IT.

Jhena, I need you. Oh, God, I need you.

Jhena Andre sat in her tiny office in the back of the administration suite. She was comparing the approved list of names for the morning's trial to the list of names vetted by the Earth Alliance Prison System. She had already compared the approved list to the list vetted through the Human Justice Division. She had five more lists to compare, and then she had to confirm that the DNA associated with the approved list of names for the morning's trial actually belonged to the person with that name.

She had stocked up on coffee: It was going to be a long night.

Jhena, please. Please.

She paused the holographic lists. The same name was highlighted on each. Behind the floating list, she could see the bare wall, the one she'd been told not to decorate since she wouldn't be here long.

Not long had gone from three weeks to six weeks to six months, and now, nearly a year. Somehow PierLuigi Frémont had managed to hire lawyers who actually argued his case, claiming at first the Earth Alliance had no jurisdiction over events in Abbondiado, and then when his lawyers had lost that, that what happened in Abbondiado had been an internal coup, not a crime against humanity.

The Criminal Court had already tossed out one of the genocide charges, saying that crimes committed on the Frontier did not belong in Earth Alliance Courts. Someone, her boss had said, was afraid of taking this case all the way to the Multicultural Tribunals, and losing.

Jhena....

She finally recognized the voice, and more importantly, she recognized the link. It was her private link, the one she'd only given to friends, and the message was encoded, which was why it seemed faint.

She cursed, and put a hand to her ear, even though she didn't need to, even though she usually made fun of people who did the very same thing.

Didier? She sent back. She knew she sounded timid, but she wasn't sure it was him. Didier Conte was the only person in the entire prison complex who could contact her on her friends link.

Yeah. Please. I need you right now. Bring evidence bags.

Evidence bags? She didn't have access to evidence bags. And then she realized that she did. Extras were stored in the closet just outside her stupid little office, along with a whole bunch of other supplies that this part of the prison needed.

Why? she sent back.

Hurry. And then he signed off.

She stared at the highlighted name, the letters blurring, the image of the person the name belonged to not really registering. Why would Didier need her? Why not call another guard? And why had he signed off so fast?

This was where she usually failed the friendship test. She didn't care what other people needed, especially if they bothered her in the middle of something.

But the something she was in the middle of was extremely tedious, and if Didier's locator was right, he was deep inside the prison, where she only got to go if a supervisor was nearby.

The prison wasn't the most dangerous one Jhena had worked at in her short twenty-one years. That would be a super max on the edge of the Earth Alliance, run by humans but housing all different kinds of aliens who'd broken human laws in various outposts along the way.

She not only couldn't go into certain parts of that prison because she would be fired; she couldn't go because she would die without the proper gear. Not everything was set up on Earth Standard. The Peyti section alone had more toxins in the atmosphere than she had seen since her childhood, when her parents were working for Ultre Corporation.

Her brain skittered away from that memory.

She stood. This was probably her only chance to see PierLuigi Frémont without dozens of guards accompanying him. Didier said that Frémont was charismatic and that made him dangerous, not that it really mattered, since it didn't matter how much the man charmed Jhena. She had no codes, no passkeys, and no DNA recognition that would allow her to open the doors to his cell.

She was quite aware of her place as a lower-level employee of the prison system, one who could be replaced with yet another machine, but wasn't partly because the law protected certain human jobs against automation, and partly because of the belief that humans could do some work better than machines.

She was grateful for the law, even though she found the belief behind it stupid. But, then, she found a lot of beliefs stupid. She'd learned to be circumspect about it, learned to use those beliefs to her benefit, like now. Even though she hated the tedium, she was getting a hell of a good paycheck, and this job was a stepping stone to better jobs elsewhere in the Earth Alliance System.

All because of a stupid belief.

She grinned, stood, and smoothed her skirt. She wasn't really dressed to go in the prisoner wing. She usually wore pants for that, and a loose-fitting shirt. Because she hadn't wanted to come to work tonight, she had made it a game, deciding to look good for once, even though no one was going to see her.

Now, it seemed, someone was. A mass murderer, by all accounts. A fascinating man. Someone famous.

She left the office, pulling the door closed behind her, and then grabbed a box of evidence bags out of the closet across the hall.

She didn't want Didier to chastise her for not bringing enough bags, so she brought too many.

She tucked the box under her arm, and headed into the high security area. She thought for a brief moment about the cameras that were everywhere, but she didn't know how to shut them off.

If she got in trouble, she would blame Didier, say that he had asked for her help, and she didn't know she wasn't supposed to give it.

But no one around here looked at the camera footage unless there was a problem.

And she hoped that despite his tone, Didier hadn't caused a problem. She hoped he just needed a little bit of help with something.

She hoped she wouldn't pay for this forever.

The thrilling adventure continues with the fifth book
in the Anniversary Day Saga, *The Peyti Crisis,*
available now from your favorite bookseller.

ABOUT THE AUTHOR

USA Today bestselling author Kristine Kathryn Rusch writes in almost every genre. Generally, she uses her real name (Rusch) for most of her writing. Under that name, she publishes bestselling science fiction and fantasy, award-winning mysteries, acclaimed mainstream fiction, controversial nonfiction, and the occasional romance. Her novels have made bestseller lists around the world and her short fiction has appeared in eighteen best of the year collections. She has won more than twenty-five awards for her fiction, including the Hugo, *Le Prix Imaginales,* the *Asimov's* Readers Choice award, and the *Ellery Queen Mystery Magazine* Readers Choice Award.

To keep up with everything she does, go to kriswrites.com. To track her many pen names and series, see their individual websites (krisnelscott.com, kristinegrayson.com, krisdelake.com, retrievalartist.com, divingintothewreck. com, fictionriver.com). She lives and occasionally sleeps in Oregon.

CPSIA information can be obtained at www.ICGtesting.com
Printed in the USA
LVOW07s2125030915

452801LV00001B/103/P